# McKenna

by Mary Casanova

★ American Girl®

*For Peyton, and all the girls at*
*Perpetual Motion Gymnastics*

Published by American Girl Publishing, Inc.
Copyright © 2012 by American Girl, LLC

Questions or comments? Call 1-800-845-0005, visit **americangirl.com**, or write to Customer Service, American Girl, 8400 Fairway Place, Middleton, WI 53562-0497.

Printed in China
12 13 14 15 16 17 18 19 LEO 10 9 8 7 6 5 4 3 2 1

All American Girl marks and McKenna™ are trademarks of American Girl, LLC.

Illustrations by Brian Hailes

Special thanks to Jeanelle Memmel; Patti Kelley Criswell, MSW; Dr. Laurie Cutting; and Dr. Debbie Staub

Cataloging-in-Publication Data available from the Library of Congress.

# Contents

Most kids don't live for gymnastics, but I do. As I hopped off the school bus, I watched my shadow lengthen on the ground before me. I practiced perfect posture—shoulders back and head held high—which made me look taller than I really am.

The September sun warmed the sidewalk outside Almost Home Coffee Shop. Bikes filled the bike rack. Customers sipped warm drinks at outdoor tables as a few dogs rested beside their owners. I headed inside and set the brass bells jingling—*ting-ting, ting-ting*. Smells of fresh-baked cookies, scones, and muffins greeted me. The coffee shop was full of customers chatting, reading, or working on laptops.

"Hi, McKenna!" said Mom, stepping out from behind the giant churning coffee roaster, her red apron tied over a skirt. Tucking strands of her sandy hair into her bun, she asked, "So, how was your *second* Tuesday of school?"

"Oh, fine," I said. "I want to start practice a little early today. Is Grandma Peg here?"

"Of course. A herd of wild horses couldn't keep her from watching you girls at gymnastics," Mom said with a grin. She tilted her head toward the break room. "Grandma is in back with Cooper and the twins. But, McKenna, before you hurry off,

1

do you have homework?"

"A little," I answered, my backpack burning with *three* unfinished assignments.

How could I tell Mom I was struggling in school, especially when my dad is a high-school principal?

As it turned out, I didn't have to say a word. Mom already knew.

"Your teacher sent an e-mail," Mom began. "He has a few concerns. Time for a 'dessert date' tonight. You, me, and Dad."

"Dessert dates" weren't always a bad thing. The last time we went on a dessert date, it was to celebrate the fact that Shooting Star Gymnastics had sent a letter inviting me to move up from Hurricanes to Twisters, the level four preteam. The letter also said that I was on track to join the competitive team next spring—something that made my heart leap. My parents and I went on a dessert date, and they asked if I wanted to keep moving up in gymnastics. My answer: "Do birds want to fly?" And then we'd toasted with milk shakes.

But now, my stomach knotted up. "Mr. Wu has concerns?" I asked. "What did he say?" I didn't know Mr. Wu very well yet, my wiry new teacher who loved to write on the board every five minutes. The first words he wrote were *Mr. Wu.* Beneath that in big letters, he wrote *WORK.* "I'm going to work you hard, fourth-graders," he had said with a sly smile. And he wasn't kidding. I could barely keep up.

"Mr. Wu has concerns about your schoolwork, McKenna," Mom said gently. "Why don't you get started on that now, and we'll talk about this later." She glanced at the round wall clock. "You have at least a half hour to do homework before you need to leave." She squeezed my shoulder and then stepped back behind the serving counter, where a new employee was working.

I chewed my bottom lip as I unzipped my backpack. I found an empty chair beneath a painting of yellow flowers and pulled out my homework. Even though Mom brought me a vanilla steamer and half a grilled cheese sandwich—which usually perked me up—I couldn't seem to focus on my science chapter. That meant I couldn't answer the worksheet that was due in class tomorrow.

I recognized the words I was reading, but their meaning went past me in a blur. So I finally gave up and turned to something I *could* do—finish up my map for social studies.

But just what exactly had Mr. Wu said in that e-mail? A sick feeling stuck between my ribs, and I caught myself staring out the window toward the harbor and Mount Rainier, frosted white in the distance.

After exactly thirty minutes—and with my homework barely started—I packed up, knocked on the break-room door, and stepped in. "There's my girl," Grandma Peg said, rising from the armchair and hugging me.

"Hi, Grandma," I said. "Mara, Maisey—time to go."

Maisey and Mara are my five-year-old twin sisters. They look alike, with big brown eyes framed by ridiculously thick eyelashes and wavy brown hair, but their personalities couldn't be more different. Grandma likes to say that "Maisey is a mover and a shaker, and Mara takes her own sweet time." And it's true. Mara was bowed over a coloring book, just starting to put her crayons away. Maisey was bouncing at the door, ready to go.

Cooper, our young golden-doodle, nearly knocked me over trying to lick my chin. I'd picked him from his litter because his energy and caramel-colored hair matched my own. "Cooper, Mom will take you out," I promised him. "And I'll walk you tomorrow, but right now, I have to go."

I couldn't wait to get to gymnastics—something that came easily to me. Ever since I was three, when I started watching gymnastics on television, it's been all I've wanted to do—especially beam.

———————★

At the gym, a hum of energy filled the air. Maisey darted off, and Mara followed to join the Twirlies group. Their teenage coach waited by the red "wedge," a foam training tool used to teach bridge kick-overs and rolls. The gym was full of equipment: two trampolines, a huge pit full of colorful foam squares—a blast to jump into!—the vault, bars, beam, and floor mats. During practice, we rotated in groups from one station to the next.

I stood by the rows of lockers and pulled off my sweats as girls of all ages arrived. Before hitting the mats, I studied the wall of photographs of gymnasts, including my coach, Isabelle Manning, former state champion. I wanted to do well at the upcoming demonstration to make her proud.

From the corner of my eye, I saw Coach Isabelle passing by, her movements as graceful as a dancer's.

I caught up with her and said, "Coach, I'm worried."

"About what, McKenna?" Isabelle asked, her dark eyebrows arched. At just a little over five feet, she isn't much taller than I am. She reached up to tuck her cropped brown hair behind her ear.

"I'm worried I won't be ready by November," I confessed. "I barely know my routines."

Isabelle laughed lightly and rested her hand on my shoulder. "Gosh, don't worry," she said. "We have about two months of practice ahead. And keep in mind, the demonstration's just for fun—a chance to see how it feels to perform before an audience. It's something to look forward to, not stress about."

From across the gym, Coach Chip Francesco shouted at one of the advanced gymnasts on the uneven bars. "Do it again!" he bellowed. "I'm pushing you because I *know* you can do it!" Pacing along the edge of the mat, Coach Chip reminded me of a restless tiger.

I liked Isabelle's "fun" approach to coaching. If I made the competitive team, Chip would be my coach. I wasn't sure how I felt about that.

"C'mon, McKenna," Isabelle said, steering me by the shoulders. "Let's get started with the others."

My eight teammates were already on the

mats, limbering up. I dropped down next to Toulane Thomas, her mink-brown hair pulled into a low side pony.

"Ready to work?" I asked, our usual greeting.

Toulane's dark, penetrating eyes met mine. "Ready to fly!" she answered with a grin.

Toulane and I are in the same class at school and have been training side by side in gymnastics since we were three-year-olds in Roly-Polies. She was the only other teammate of mine who was invited to try out for the competitive team next spring. Ever since we'd received our letters, Toulane had been extra competitive at the gym, but that was okay. She always pushed *me* to do my best, too.

I thought of the e-mail Mr. Wu sent my parents. What did it matter if I was falling a little behind at school? I'd catch up soon enough. Right now, I was at gymnastics, and it was time to fly!

"Level-four girls," Coach Isabelle announced, walking toward us with a lanky, red-headed girl, "I want you to meet our newest member, Sierra Kuchinko. She comes from a club in San Francisco."

I recognized Sierra from school. She was in the other fourth-grade class, but she looked older because she was about a foot taller than the rest of us. While the other girls took turns introducing themselves, Toulane leaned toward me and whispered, "She's really big. I bet she's flexible as a rock."

"Bet she's strong," I countered.

When it was Toulane's turn, she jumped up. "Hi. I'm Toulane," she said, and then she launched into three cartwheels in rapid succession.

Not to be outdone, I sprang to my feet. "Hi, Sierra. I'm McKenna," I said with a wave. "Glad you're on our team." Then I threw myself into the same routine as Toulane's and added a straddle jump at the end.

Isabelle wagged her finger at us, but she was smiling. "Okay, you two," she scolded playfully. "You know it's not time for floorwork yet. Up the ropes!"

Rope climbing is sometimes used as a punishment, but I know that Isabelle also uses it to help gymnasts build upper-body strength.

"Race you to the top!" Toulane whispered, standing at the base of her rope.

"You're on!" I shot back, grabbing my own rope.

Hand over hand, muscles burning the higher I climbed, I reached the red ball at the top—at the same instant as Toulane. Then I gripped the rope loosely between my hands and feet and started working my way back down.

We reached the mats at the same moment, and Toulane glanced over at the rows of folding chairs for her mom. I spotted Grandma, who raised her hands over her head and clapped silently, sending "love beams" my way. She said that was her way of over-coming her worries that I might get hurt.

I noticed that Toulane's mother wasn't looking at us at all. She was busy watching Toulane's older sister, Tasha, on the competitive team. I saw a flash of hurt in Toulane's eyes as she looked away from her mother and back at me.

When Toulane and I joined the group again on the mats, the new girl, Sierra, was stretching into a perfect side splits.

Toulane and I exchanged an envious glance. Neither of us could stretch that far!

The hour-and-a-half practice flew by as we

rotated by groups through the various stations. As always, practice ended all too soon.

When Grandma pulled her red Jeep into our driveway to drop us off, she turned off the engine. "It seems I'm staying with the twins for a bit this evening," she said, patting my knee and giving me a supportive smile.

During gymnastics I'd been able to forget about the dessert date ahead, but now my stomach twisted at the reminder. I was trying my best at school, but it wasn't good enough, and I still had unfinished homework waiting for me.

After a chicken pasta dinner, Dad pushed back his chair and removed his thick black glasses. "Well, McKenna," he said, blowing on his glasses and cleaning them with the edge of his denim shirt, "let's rock 'n' roll. And bring your backpack."

*Rock 'n' roll.* It's what Dad often says when he's trying to get us girls out the door.

Our house is in the Queen Anne neighborhood, close to downtown Seattle, so my parents and I hopped on our bikes and in minutes were at Sparky's, a tiny new restaurant with orange-cushioned chairs. The minute after we ordered, Dad pulled out his cell phone and started reading Mr. Wu's e-mail—*out loud!*

11

"Dad. Whisper, please!" I begged him.

"Sure, McKenna. Sorry," he said, much more quietly. He started reading again:

*Dear Mr. and Mrs. Brooks,*

*McKenna's records show that she has done very well in school in the past, but I have a few concerns as she starts this year. I've noticed that she's not finishing some of her assignments on time.*

*I'm hoping that we can meet as soon as possible to discuss strategies for helping McKenna get back on track. I know she can do it!*

*Sincerely, Mr. Wu*

I slumped in my seat. "My teacher must think I'm a loser," I groaned.

"We all know you're not a loser, McKenna," said Mom, lowering her chin to look me in the eye. Then she asked about my homework. "Show us what you're working on exactly."

I pulled out two textbooks and a few worksheets. I couldn't fake it a day longer. "I don't know what's happening this year," I admitted.

I handed the worksheets to Mom as the waiter placed desserts in front of us. I love Mud Fudge cake, but now I wasn't sure I could eat a single bite.

As my parents reviewed my homework, they asked more questions. Finally, Dad ran the flat palm of his hand front to back over his nearly bald head. I knew that meant he had something serious to say. "McKenna, I know you don't want to hear this," he said, "but in order to bring your grades up, you may have to pull back on gymnastics. It has to be school first and gymnastics second."

My stomach clenched. *Pull back on gymnastics?* Gymnastics is my life! My bedroom walls are decorated with posters of my favorite gymnasts. Plus I have sticky notes all over my room with messages written on them like "Never give up!" and "If you can believe it, you can achieve it!" Had my parents forgotten what gymnastics means to me?

"But, Dad, true athletes give up *everything* to be at the top," I said, my voice rising.

"Yes," he said, "and some never finish high school or college, either. But that's not going to be you."

"Dad. I'm only in fourth grade," I protested, but I could already tell I was losing this battle.

Mom leaned in closer. "Y'know, McKenna," she said, "I left the corporate world to run the coffee shop because it's closer to home. I had to reset my priorities to family first, work second. And you know what?"

"What?" I asked flatly.

"I see you girls so much more now," said Mom. "And I'm happier."

"But I'm happy doing *gymnastics*," I said in frustration. I felt as if I were talking to aliens.

"Gymnastics is important to you," Dad went on. "We get that. But schoolwork should be, too. If you can find a way to do both, great. But school has to come first. We're going to try to set up a time to talk with your teacher later this week."

I didn't know what to say. I sighed and then stifled a yawn.

"It's getting late," Dad said. "Time to rock 'n' roll."

That night at home, I stayed up until I finished my homework. It was stressful, but tackling it at my desk helped. My desk is a cozy place, tucked under my loft bed. In the warm glow of lamplight, I can see my bulletin board filled with photos, cards, and notes from friends and family. On the shelf to my left is a clock and my favorite books.

And there's Polka Dot.

*Creak, creak, creak.*

My brown and white hamster raced on her

squeaky wheel in her cage.

Cooper padded into my room, too, stole a lick of my chin, and then curled up on his dog bed with a deep doggy sigh.

"I know, boy," I said. "I'm tired, too." I turned off my lamp and climbed the ladder to my bed. I lay on my back, took a deep breath, and exhaled. To help us deal with stress, Coach Isabelle had taught the team to breathe in our favorite colors slowly—always sky blue for me—and then exhale slowly.

*Blue sky in . . . gray sky out.*

I did the breathing exercise two or three more times, but I still wasn't sure I could sleep.

I propped myself up on my elbow and peeked at Cooper from over the rail of my bed, where I usually feel as if I'm on top of the world. Cooper opened one eye and thumped his tail to show that he was listening.

"I have to do better at school, Cooper," I whispered down to him. "But what if I *can't?*"

Two days later, while our class was working on multiplication problems, I went to sharpen my pencil near the front of the room. Mr. Wu motioned to me to step closer to his desk.

"McKenna," he said quietly, "I know you're having a tough time with school—that's why I sent the e-mail to your parents. But keep working at it, okay? It's important for your future."

"Okay," I said softly. I couldn't look at him. Hoping no one else had heard Mr. Wu's words, I returned to my desk, my face flushed.

Toulane, who sat across from me, whispered, "What was that about?"

"Oh, nothing," I said as casually as I could.

"It's never nothing," Toulane insisted. Her intense brown eyes searched mine for clues.

I shrugged and looked away.

As we pulled out our reading assignment, I tried to focus on the words. Pretty soon, though, my mind was drifting. I imagined becoming a famous gymnast . . . bending my head to accept the gold medal. If I could see it and believe it, I could achieve it. But how was I supposed to work harder at school when it was so *boring* compared to gymnastics?

"McKenna?" Mr. Wu said. "Please turn to

page 17 with the rest of the class."

"Yes, Mr. Wu," I said, my face on fire again.

Near the end of the day, Mr. Wu stood before us clapping his hands to get our attention. "Time for the science test I warned you about," he said. He reached for the stack of tests and began passing them out. "The answers are all in that first chapter."

That first chapter had put me to sleep, and it hadn't made any sense. What if I bombed this test? "I don't get this stuff," I whispered to myself.

Something nudged me between my shoulder blades. I turned around in my chair and saw Elizabeth Onishi, her pale face framed by black bangs, holding up the eraser end of her pencil. Elizabeth and I aren't close friends, but we get along pretty well, and she lives just down the street from me. "You'll do fine," she whispered.

"Thanks," I said, mustering a smile.

*Blue sky in . . . gray sky out.*

As the clock ticked toward the end of the school day, however, everyone had finished the test—except me. My face burned hotter and hotter, like red coals.

Mr. Wu must have noticed. He knelt beside me and said, "Just take it home to finish it."

"Thanks, Mr. Wu," I whispered.

He was being really nice, but somehow that just made me feel worse. Was I the only student in the class who needed special treatment?

———★

That night at the gym, I worked extra hard on my floor routine, getting lost in the music. Moving on to the bar, I felt like a bird—soaring, stretching, and flying.

When it was time for the vault, I pictured myself doing a perfect handstand flat-back skill. Then I set off down the runway, jumped onto the springboard, and rose up into a handstand on the vault. I held the position tight and then pushed over and landed with a flat back on the stack of thick mats. *Did it!*

I ended practice on the beam, sticking my landing. *Yes!*

It was a perfect night at the gym—a reminder of why I *love* gymnastics. Grandma clapped silently from the viewing area. Sierra complimented me, too. "Nice landing," she said. "And great form."

"Thanks!" I said, smiling broadly.

"Landings are something my other coach

drilled us on," said Sierra. She stood up straight and pursed her lips. "You must *work* on lengthening your neck, like a *dancer*. Like a *swan!*" With great exaggeration, Sierra threw her arms out to her sides and flung her head back.

I imitated her. "Like a *swan!*" I said, assuming the same position. Then we cracked up and couldn't stop laughing.

Toulane was on beam now, toes pointed. She shot us a jealous glance. "Hey, McKenna, I'm not done yet," she said. "Will you watch me?"

"Sure," I said. As I stepped toward the beam, I turned and waved good-bye to Sierra.

Later that night, after I finished doing dinner dishes, Maisey and Mara tugged the legs of my jeans. "Watch us do cartwheels!" Maisey insisted.

"Please?" added Mara.

"I have homework," I said, glancing at the kitchen clock. It was already 6:45. But I knew my sisters wouldn't stop begging until I watched them do cartwheels, so I took a few minutes with them in their jungle-decorated bedroom.

Maisey announced, "I'm faster. Watch!" Beaming, she flipped end over end.

"No, I'm faster," Mara said. She pushed her

shoulders back, breathed deeply, and then cartwheeled in slow motion. When she finished, she stretched out her arms and arched her head back, her expression proud.

"Great! Nice job, you two!" I said, applauding. When they started arguing about who had done the better cartwheel, I slipped away to my bedroom and sat down at my desk.

Polka Dot stopped running on her wheel for a second and looked at me, her pink nose twitching. Then she took off again at full speed. "Can't you give it a rest, Polka Dot, just for a few minutes?" I asked, exasperated. But she couldn't. Polka Dot loves her wheel as much as I love gymnastics.

I turned to my homework and pulled out the science test. My stomach tightened, just as it had in class, and a wave of anxiety swept over me. *What was wrong with me?*

I stared at the test questions. I still had nine to answer! I took a deep breath and told myself that if I just worked hard, I could get this done. And I could get a grip on my other homework, too. It was early in the year, right? I'd never love homework, but if I wanted to stay in gymnastics, I had better try harder.

I tried—really tried—to find the answers in the

textbook. But I kept thinking of laughing with Sierra at the gym, and my eyes danced over the words. After a half hour of trying, I'd answered only two more questions. I felt like Polka Dot on her wheel—running in circles and not getting anywhere!

I couldn't go to school tomorrow with the take-home test half done—or, worse yet, with a bunch of wrong answers. I twirled my pencil and thought of Elizabeth Onishi. Elizabeth lived only six houses down from ours, and she was a good student. She might be willing to help me. I wouldn't ask for answers outright—just a few hints.

I carefully folded the test into quarters and then folded it again and tucked it into my back pocket.

"Mom, Dad—" I said, stepping into the hallway, "I'm taking Cooper for a walk!"

At the word *walk*, Cooper bounded to me, tail wagging.

Dad glanced up from the couch. "He'll like that," he said. "Thank you. But keep it short, okay? It'll be dark soon."

Mom was napping, her feet on Dad's lap and her head on the other end of the couch. She often falls asleep early after getting up at the crack of dawn to open the coffee shop.

With Cooper on a leash, I headed out the front door and down the porch steps. I walked the long way around the block before stopping at Elizabeth's brick two-story house. Cooper sniffed the tidy shrubs along the sidewalk, and I had to pull him with me up to Elizabeth's front door. Before I lost my nerve, I pressed the doorbell.

Elizabeth answered the door, her hair pulled back into a messy bun. "Hey, McKenna," she said. "What's up?"

"Um, well, I didn't exactly finish the science test today," I stammered, "and Mr. Wu said I could take it home to finish it. But I'm stuck, and I thought maybe . . . you could give me . . . a little help."

"Sure!" said Elizabeth, stepping outside to join me and Cooper. "I can just give you the answers, if you'd like. Which ones don't you know?"

"Um," I hesitated. I didn't want to cheat, but I was running out of time. If Elizabeth was willing to give me the answers, well . . . I pulled my test out of my pocket.

Just then Mrs. Onishi appeared in the doorway. She glanced at my test and raised one eyebrow. That's when I knew we were in trouble.

"Girls!" she scolded. "A *test* means you need to do your own work, right?"

"But, Mom," piped up Elizabeth, "it's more like a quiz. It isn't a big deal."

My tongue was glued to the roof of my dry mouth. My cheeks burned hotter than jalapeños! I couldn't move a single muscle.

"Well, getting answers for a quiz isn't okay either," said Mrs. Onishi. "It's *cheating*. Elizabeth, you and I are going to talk about this further. McKenna, should I tell your parents about this—or will you?"

I wanted to say *I'm really not a cheater, but I got stuck and couldn't do the work, and there's gymnastics, and . . .* But I knew those would all sound like flimsy excuses. The fact was, I had been willing to get the answers from Elizabeth—to cheat. My eyes filled with tears. I dreaded the idea of telling my parents.

From the oak tree in the front lawn, a gray squirrel began scolding in a high-pitched chatter. Cooper yanked hard on his leash toward the tree, jolting me off center.

"Um," I said, my tongue finally loosening, "I'll tell them."

# Chapter 4

# The Fourth-Grade Slump

Cooper and I shuffled around the block, taking the long way home. I couldn't have walked any slower. I had to tell my parents, but how could I? By the time I reached our front porch, my feet felt as heavy as ship anchors. Somehow, I climbed the steps and pushed through the front door.

"How was your walk?" Dad asked brightly.

I took a deep breath. I figured I had better tell my parents the truth right away, before I lost my nerve—or before Mara and Maisey came bounding into the room.

"Mom, Dad, I have to tell you something," I said quickly. I flopped cross-legged on the floor beside the couch and told them everything as fast as I could get it out. When I finished, my eyes were red and my nose was running.

"Here," Mom said gently, handing me a tissue from the coffee table.

"McKenna," Dad said, "you know cheating is wrong. There are no shortcuts to learning. For punishment, perhaps you need to take a week off from gymnastics."

"A whole week?" I groaned. "I'll fall way behind!"

"But, McKenna," said Dad, "that's what's

happening at school."

"Yes, but . . ." I began. My chin trembled and I tried to keep from crying again. "I'm trying really hard! I am, but I just . . . can't . . . get it."

Mom leaned over to put her arm around my shoulder. "Sweetheart," she said, "if you're really trying but you're still struggling, it's definitely time to get some help." She glanced up at Dad, and something passed between them. Sometimes it's as if they have their own language.

Dad nodded at Mom and then turned back to me. "McKenna," he began again, more softly this time, "we have a meeting set up with Mr. Wu after school tomorrow. If you're willing to work with your mom, me, and your new teacher to get some help with your schoolwork, we'll allow you to stick with practice—at least for now. Fair enough?"

I couldn't speak over the lump in my throat. All I could do was nod my head.

My parents stayed up late with me and had me read the whole science chapter out loud to them. I had to read some paragraphs more than once, but I finally answered all of the test questions.

As I crawled into bed, I thought about meeting with my parents and Mr. Wu tomorrow. I wasn't crazy about the idea, but I wasn't going to put up a fuss. If this was the only way to stay in gymnastics, I'd do it.

———————★

Friday morning at school, a dark, gloomy cloud hovered over our classroom. Right away, Mr. Wu told us to take out our library books. "You can read silently while I work with each of you, one at a time, in the hallway," he explained.

Mr. Wu pulled a couple of chairs into the hallway. When it was my turn to join him, I read a few paragraphs aloud, the words tumbling off my tongue, while he listened and timed me with a stopwatch.

"Nice, McKenna. You read aloud beautifully," he said.

I smiled with relief. "Thanks," I said.

"Now tell me what you just read," said Mr. Wu.

*Uh-oh.* I hadn't really been paying attention. "Um, something about pelicans," I said hesitantly.

"And?" he pressed.

I panicked. I honestly didn't know. "Oil slicks?" I asked.

"Oil slicks can be a real problem for wildlife, but that wasn't part of this text," said Mr. Wu. "Do you remember reading anything about wingspan?

Or what pelicans eat?"

I tried to pretend that the answers were right there on the tip of my tongue. Mr. Wu waited. Finally, I just shrugged. "If I read it again . . . " I suggested.

Mr. Wu smiled gently and shook his head. "That's okay," he said. "I think I know why you've been struggling with your schoolwork, McKenna."

"Why?" I asked, partly curious and partly dreading his response.

"You have trouble with *reading comprehension,* or understanding what you're reading," said Mr. Wu.

*Reading?* I was shocked. Reading had always seemed easy. Why would it be hard for me now?

"Lots of fourth-graders struggle with the same thing," Mr. Wu continued, as if reading my mind. "And now that we know, I'll be better able to help you."

When I returned to my desk, I looked around, wondering who else was struggling with reading comprehension. Elizabeth always had her nose in a book, so I figured reading was easy for her. Plus, she wasn't in a sport, so she had more time for homework.

I glanced at Toulane across the aisle from me. Maybe she was struggling, too, because of gymnastics practices.

"Toulane," I whispered, leaning across the

aisle. "Tough science test yesterday, huh?"

Toulane looked at me as if I'd asked the silliest question in the world. "No, it wasn't bad," she said.

I flushed and sat back in my chair. "Yeah," I mumbled. "Just kidding."

Clearly, not everyone in my class was having as much trouble as I was.

⎯⎯★

At the end of the school day, Dad and Mom showed up to meet Mr. Wu. We sat in the reading area on an overstuffed purple couch.

"McKenna and I talked a little bit today about the difficulties she's been having with homework," Mr. Wu explained. "I think she's struggling with reading comprehension."

Mom's brow furrowed. "I'm surprised," she said. "McKenna has always sailed through school."

Mr. Wu nodded. "We call this the 'fourth-grade slump,'" he said. "Through third grade, students focus on learning to read. But fourth grade places more emphasis on 'reading to learn.' It's a time when reading difficulties often arise."

"Mm-hmm," Dad said in agreement. Then he added, "As principal of the high school, I'm familiar with a few tutoring options. In fact, the middle school has a peer tutoring program where older students work with younger students. Is that something that might help McKenna?"

Mr. Wu lit up. "I'm sure we could find an excellent student to work with McKenna," he agreed.

None of this made any sense to me. It felt worse than messing up a routine at the gym! "A reading *tutor*?" I said out loud, staring at my shoes.

"Exactly," said Mr. Wu. "Let's see what we can arrange." He stepped out of the classroom to walk down to the office. When he returned, he was all smiles. "All set, McKenna. You'll have a sixth-grade tutor on Mondays and Wednesdays at the school library. Her name's Josie Myers."

"Really?" said Mom. "Her mother owns a drapery business downtown, near my coffee shop."

Mr. Wu nodded at Mom and then turned back to me. "So, McKenna, all you need to do is leave class thirty minutes early on those days," he explained. "What do you think?"

I was mortified. "But what if other kids find out?" I asked softly, more to myself than to anyone else. "They'll think—they'll think I have problems."

"If you want to tell others, that's up to you,"

said Mr. Wu. "I won't say anything. But remember, McKenna, there's nothing wrong with trying new things and getting a little help."

Mom pointed out to Mr. Wu that I was always learning new skills at Shooting Star Gymnastics.

"Is that so?" Mr. Wu said. "Who's your coach?"

"Isabelle Manning," I answered, my voice stronger now that I was talking about gymnastics.

"Think you'd make progress without her help?" asked Mr. Wu.

I thought about that and shook my head. "No," I admitted. "Not much."

"You're lucky," said Mr. Wu. "Isabelle is an excellent athlete—and coach. She knows her stuff."

"Wait, you know her?" I asked, leaning forward.

"I was a gymnast," said Mr. Wu, with what I thought was a hint of pride. "Great sport, McKenna. Try to think of your tutor as kind of like a gymnastics coach. Instead of getting help learning gymnastics, you're getting coaching in reading."

A reading tutor like a gymnastics coach? *Uh, I don't think so.*

———————★

Saturday morning, I rolled out of bed early

for gymnastics. As I arrived at the gym, just behind Sierra, Isabelle handed us each a sheet of paper. "Take this with you and memorize it," she said.

I pulled off my sweats and then paused by my locker to study the sheet, which read:

REQUIRED ELEMENTS FOR
LEVEL 4 COMPETITIVE TEAM

ON VAULT: handstand flat back onto a mat stack

ON BARS: glide swing, pullover, front hip circle, shoot-through, stride circle, single leg cut, cast, back hip circle to underswing dismount

ON BEAM: v-sit, heel-snap turn in coupé, leap, handstand, half turn in coupé, straight jump, tuck jump, scale, side handstand quarter-turn dismount

ON FLOOR: straight jump, split jump, handstand forward roll, handstand bridge kick-over, leap, hop, split, back roll to push-up position, half turn in coupé, round-off back handspring rebound

For me, reading anything about gymnastics was as easy as reading the ABCs. I could picture each and every move—not only picture it but also feel it. Then I flashed on that awful take-home test. Why was *that* so tough?

"The last gym I was at," Sierra said, "was just for fun. But moving here and up to Level 4—it's intense, isn't it?"

"Yeah, it is," I agreed. *That's why I love it,* I wanted to add. I was always scared facing a new move, but then when I tried—and eventually succeeded—it was exciting to discover what I could do.

As I stood side by side with Sierra, the difference in our height was suddenly more noticeable. As if reading my thoughts, Sierra blurted, "Y'know, I'm big for fourth grade. But it's because of my dad."

"How so?" I asked.

"Well, I'm tall like him," Sierra explained. "He's six and a half feet tall!" Sierra didn't sound very happy about that. "My parents got divorced, and I had to move here with my mom," she added, but then quickly looked down at the floor. "I don't know why I told you that. You seem nice, I guess."

Sierra's words made me feel pretty good—as if we were already friends. "Thanks for telling me," I said. "And there's nothing wrong with being tall."

Sierra shrugged. "I guess I just feel like a giant compared to the rest of you," she said sadly.

"Hey, you fit right in," I said quickly, trying to reassure her. "We're teammates!"

"But you guys are way ahead of me when it comes to all this stuff," said Sierra, holding up the orange list of gymnastics moves. "How am I going to remember all this?"

"I'll help you," I said—and I meant it. "You'll catch up in no time." Then I tapped the side of my head. "As Coach always says, 'Girls, it all starts here!'"

Sierra laughed, so maybe I had already helped her—at least a little bit.

While we stretched on the mats, I waited for Toulane to show up, but she never did. It wasn't like her to miss gymnastics. I wondered if she was sick.

As we moved from the mats to the trampoline, though, I forgot about Toulane, take-home tests, and tutors. I loved jumping high, feeling my body fly into the air and leaving everything else behind.

That afternoon, I brought my homework with me into the backyard and spread it all out on a blanket in the grass. Horns sounded from the distant harbor. A breeze ruffled the mums, a garden of rusty reds and golds. The afternoon stretched out long before me, with plenty of time for studying. I was determined to get my work done—period.

I opened my social studies book to the chapter about the Oregon Trail and started reading about early pioneers making the impossible journey from the East Coast to the West. I read the first few paragraphs, but as I turned the page, I couldn't remember what I'd read. I started over. The third time through, my little sisters' singing shattered my concentration.

"I'm a little teapot, short and stout," they sang from the playhouse Grandpa Jack had built for them.

"Maisey! Mara! I'm doing *homework*," I stressed to them. "Can you please keep it down?"

But Mara continued singing as she leaned out the playhouse window, her arm pointing forward like a teakettle spout. Maisey leaned out the doorway, her arm curved in the shape of a handle. As soon as they finished their song, Maisey called, "Oh, Miss! Come for tea!"

"Today's special," Mara added, "is extra special.

It's Chinese green tea all the way from China."

I groaned. "Okay, I'm coming," I finally said. If I visited, maybe they would leave me alone afterward.

After drinking my tea—water served in a tiny teacup—I gave up my idea of studying outside and returned to my bedroom.

*Ah, quiet.* I had my room to myself.

I settled at my desk and read three pages, but my brain felt like a dry ocean sponge—absorbing *nothing* of what I had just read. I started over again.

Polka Dot woke up and headed for her wheel. *Creak, creak, creak.*

This time as I read, instead of thinking about the challenges of the Oregon Trail, I replayed the Level 4 gymnastics elements in my mind. Studying was hopeless.

Maybe I *did* need a tutor after all.

When Dad called me to set the table for dinner, I stepped into the hallway and stumbled over Cooper. His head was burrowed inside my gymnastics bag just outside my door. I pulled the bag away from Cooper and saw immediately what he had done. There, just inside the opening of the bag, were my leather grips—chewed into shreds and covered with Cooper drool.

"Not my new grips!" I cried. "Bad dog!"

Cooper slunk around the hallway corner into the kitchen. I followed him, carrying the evidence. Cooper cowered by Dad's legs in front of the stove.

"McKenna," Dad said, pulling a casserole from the oven, "he's still a pup. He's going to do things like that, especially if he's bored."

"But, Dad—they're my new grips!" I protested, glaring at Cooper.

"After dinner," said Dad calmly, "you and I are taking him on a long walk."

<hr>

The walk helped clear my head. Dad has a way of always making me feel things will be okay. He said he'd replace the grips before Tuesday's practice. "It's partly my fault," he said. "We ran out of chews for him, and I forgot to pick some up."

"And I shouldn't have left my bag on the floor," I admitted. I got why Cooper did what he did. After all, I was pretty bored, too, trying to wade through homework. But why did Cooper have to chew up my grips—something I needed for gymnastics? Part of me wished he'd chewed up my *homework* instead.

On Sunday afternoon, Grandma Peg and Grandpa Jack came over for a barbecue.

"How're my girls?" Grandpa asked, greeting each of us with a kiss on the cheek. Grandpa smelled like soap, and his white mustache and beard were scratchy on my face. I pretended to brush his bristly kiss off my cheek. It was our game.

Grandpa laughed. "What?" he teased. "You don't like my whiskers?"

"Nooo!" the twins sang.

"No," I said, "but I like you."

"I know you do," he said warmly as he ruffled my hair.

Smoke rose from the backyard grill as we gathered around the picnic table. Grandpa jiggled the edge of the table with his large hands. "A little loose," he announced. "I'll tighten it up before we sit down." And then he was off to rummage around in our garage for a tool.

After a dinner of salmon and corn on the cob, Grandma sank into a lounge chair. "Oh, I ate too much," she said. "How about if you girls entertain me?"

I never refused an invitation to show off my gymnastics moves, even though I had to share the grass stage with Mara and Maisey. After a solid ten minutes of performing, Grandma motioned us to her side. "Girls, come here," she called.

I stood beside her and touched her short, wavy hair. Grandma keeps saying she's going to color her hair to get rid of the "winter white," but I like it. I love her blue eyes, too, which match my own.

From a small bag beside her chair, Grandma pulled out three tiny boxes. "I want you each to know," she said sweetly, "that no matter what, you are all stars to me—and always will be."

My sisters tore into their boxes, but I took my time. We each pulled out a silver necklace with a star pendant.

"Stars for my stars," Grandma said. "Here, let me help." She tried putting the necklace around my neck. "Oh, these darn fingers," she finally said. "A little arthritis and they just don't want to cooperate."

I had noticed that Grandma's fingers were getting a little more lumpy and curvy. "That's okay, Grandma," I said to her. "I can do it."

As I fastened the clasp on my star necklace, Mom helped my sisters with theirs. Then I gave Grandma a huge hug. "Oh, Grandma," I said, squeezing her, "thank you!"

I loved the necklace. It would help remind me that Grandma was cheering for me—always.

———★

Despite the star necklace twinkling from around my neck, Monday was a long day at school. Two things were weighing heavily on my mind.

First, Toulane told me that she had missed gymnastics because her sister, Tasha, had been in a bike accident. Tasha had been hurt pretty badly. She was going to be okay, but she probably wouldn't be able to come back to gymnastics, at least not anytime soon. I kept thinking how hard that would be—to have to give up something I loved so much.

The other gray cloud hanging over my head was my afternoon meeting with a tutor. Ugh!

The clock ticked along minute by minute. As it closed in on 2:30—thirty minutes before the end of class—I packed my backpack with schoolwork, wishing I were invisible.

Toulane shot me a look. "McKenna," she whispered, "why do *you* get to leave early?"

I certainly wasn't going to tell her the truth! And I didn't have a good excuse—or lie. I just shrugged my shoulders, rose from my desk, and with a nod of approval from Mr. Wu, headed for the classroom door.

"Where's she going?" someone else asked.

I felt all eyes on my back as Mr. Wu said, "Class, it's not your concern. McKenna has a special meeting."

My footsteps echoed as I hurried down the hall and pushed through the double-wide doors to the school library. Mr. Hornbauer looked over his glasses from the main desk. "Hi, McKenna," he said. "Josie's here already."

Did *everyone* know I needed a tutor?

I glanced around the room for someone who might be standing taller than me—a sixth-grader. But then I noticed a golden-haired girl seated beside a library table, parked in a wheelchair.

"Hi, are you McKenna?" she asked. Her voice was friendly and confident, and her dimples deepened with her smile, but I wanted to bolt. The last thing I had expected was someone in a wheelchair.

"You're my . . . my tutor?" I stammered.

"Yeah," she replied. "I mean, if you *want* one." Her smile started to fade.

Why hadn't Mr. Wu warned me? I felt a rush of embarrassment. I'd never talked to someone in a

wheelchair before. If this girl couldn't walk, I didn't know what else to expect. Maybe she couldn't talk or think clearly, either. My feet were glued to the library carpet. I wanted to turn around, head back to my classroom, and tell Mr. Wu, "There must be some mistake!"

Then I reminded myself: *no tutor, no gymnastics.* I willed myself forward.

The girl tilted her head, as if she could read my thoughts. "Hey, I'm Josie," she said. "And this is my wheelchair, Lightning."

"Lightning?" I repeated.

"I figure it's the closest I'll ever get to riding a horse," she said with a grin, "so, yeah—Lightning. Sounds horsey, doesn't it?"

I didn't know what to think of this tutor. "I guess," I said.

"You ever ride a horse?" she asked brightly.

"Uh, nope," I said, shaking my head.

"Me neither," she admitted with a sigh. "Still, I dream about it. Problem is"—she nodded toward her legs—"these aren't exactly cowgirl legs."

I felt myself relax a little. I almost smiled.

Then Josie got down to business. "Have a seat," she said. "Let's start with whatever homework you've got." She eyed my backpack. "Ever feel like a turtle carrying that around on your back every day?"

I shrugged. Honestly? I felt more like tucking my head into my shell than talking with her. I knew Josie was trying to get me to open up, but I just couldn't do it.

I glanced at the library doors. School wasn't out yet. What if someone I knew came in and saw me getting help?

Josie paused for a moment and then said, "Hey, I know this probably isn't easy for you."

I sighed and finally sank into a chair beside her. "The truth is," I said, trying to find the right words, "the only reason I'm doing this is . . ."

"Let me guess," said Josie. "It's because you *have* to, right?"

I nodded. "So I can stay in gymnastics," I explained to her.

"Oh, gymnastics!" said Josie, sounding genuinely interested. "I bet you have to do a lot of training for that."

"Three days a week," I told her. "My coach says that's the only way to stay strong and flexible." The words were flowing from my mouth now that we were talking about something *interesting*.

"I don't do gymnastics," said Josie, "but studying is kind of like a workout. I figure we have to stretch and work out our brains the same way we do with our bodies."

*Work out my brain?* I'd never really thought about that. Maybe strength and flexibility were important for learning at school, too. Hmm . . . I could already tell that this Josie girl was pretty smart.

I opened my backpack, willing to give my brain a good stretch—and my tutor a chance. But at that very moment, someone from my class strolled into the library. It was Elizabeth Onishi with an armload of books. She headed to the main desk, not yet having spotted me.

"This library can't keep up with you, Elizabeth," Mr. Hornbauer exclaimed. "You're such a voracious reader!"

Now I really wanted to disappear—like Polka Dot into her den.

I slid off my chair and hurried behind a stack of books, pretending to take a sudden interest in books about dinosaurs. Through the shelf opening, I watched until Elizabeth left through the library doors—*phew!* Then I walked back to the table and plunked down.

Josie leaned toward me. "Wow, what was *that* all about?" she asked.

"Oh, I wanted to look at some books for a science project," I lied. I couldn't meet Josie's eyes, because I was afraid that if I did, she'd know the truth—that I was embarrassed to be seen being tutored, especially by a tutor who looked so, well, *different.*

During Wednesday's tutoring session, I kept one eye on the library doors, hoping that no one else I knew would walk in. Josie must have thought I was bored, because she said, "Y'know, McKenna, when we finish early, we can do other fun stuff."

"Like what?" I asked her.

"I'll get more ideas as we go from my teacher," she said, "but for now, let's try this." She turned to a nearby shelf and grabbed a book, not showing me the title. "I'm going to read the opening page of a novel, and you tell me where you think the story's going. Your job is to predict what happens to this character."

"Just one page?" I asked.

"Yup," she said, flipping to the first page of the book. She began reading aloud about a baby boy named Tristan who was dropped off at an abbey in the middle of the night, along with a royal letter. It was fun listening to Josie read. She read smoothly and with lots of drama in her voice. When she reached the end of the page, she stopped reading and asked me, "What do you think happens next?"

"Well," I said hesitantly, "it sounds as if some powerful person wants this boy dead. And he'll have to work hard to stay alive. Maybe he's a prince?"

"Good!" said Josie. Then she showed me the

cover of the book. It was called *The Youngest Templar.*
"Your turn now," said Josie. "Read something to me."

I chose *The Penderwicks.* As I read the first page,
Josie watched me with attentive eyes. As soon as I
finished the page, she said, "Hmm. If these sisters
talked 'for a long time' about their summer at this
place, Arundel, then I predict . . . the sisters are going
to have some great adventures ahead—and probably
get into some kind of trouble, too."

We took turns reading first pages of novels to
each other and predicting what might happen to the
main characters. We went on like this through half a
dozen books. It was like a game. I liked thinking of
where the author might take the story after the first
page. With some books, the very first sentence really
got me thinking—and predicting.

When we stopped, Josie said, "You did great!
Okay, here's a tough one: Let's predict our futures.
You go first."

"You mean like tomorrow, or in twenty years?"
I asked her.

"Whichever," she said. "I'm just curious."

I'd never really thought much beyond gymnastics. "Well," I began, "I predict . . . doing well at
the gymnastics demonstration in November and then

making the competitive team next spring."

"And when you're grown up?" Josie asked.

I flashed to the image of myself wearing a gold medal, but I didn't tell Josie about that dream. "I really don't know," I said. "How about you? What do you predict for your future?"

Josie said, "Well, I was thinking I'd become a famous ballerina." She glanced at me sideways and then laughed.

I laughed, too. Josie had a great sense of humor, which made me feel more comfortable around her.

"No," she said, "actually I think I'd like to be a researcher—the first one to find a cure for something."

"Like what?" I asked.

"Anything," she said. "Maybe for paralysis so that I can finally use my legs."

I glanced uncomfortably at Josie's legs—the first time I'd really looked. Though she wore jeans and tennis shoes, her legs and feet seemed a little smaller than the rest of her. I caught myself staring. "I'm sorry—for staring," I said quickly. "I mean, um, I don't know what to say. I'm sorry about your legs."

Josie tossed her head and smiled, as if telling me not to worry. "Thanks," she said, "but it's not your fault. I was born this way, so I can't blame anyone, really. I used to feel sorry for myself. I felt as if I had this huge mountain to climb. But finally, with lots of help from my mom and dad, I realized that it was up to me, that the only way I was going to get to the top of that mountain was one step, or roll,"—she added, grinning and tapping her wheelchair—"at a time."

I smiled back at Josie. I didn't know what to say. She seemed so brave—and so smart. After an awkward silence, I glanced at the clock. Even though we had ten minutes left, I started gathering my things. I was hoping to leave the library before class got out. I didn't want to run into anyone I knew while Josie was tutoring me.

"I need to leave a little early today," I said, standing up to go. "Thanks for your help today, Josie. I had fun."

Josie looked surprised that I was leaving so soon, but she just shrugged and said, "Okay, McKenna. See you Monday."

———————★

The next afternoon at the gym, my Level 4 group was practicing handstand bridge kick-overs, but Sierra kept toppling. When Toulane chuckled,

I tried to think of something encouraging to say to Sierra. I thought of Josie's words in the library yesterday.

I motioned Sierra aside. "Sierra," I said, "think of doing a kick-over as climbing a mountain one step at a time. Just go slow, and keep breathing."

The next time Sierra attempted the move, she slowed down and actually completed the element without wiping out. Her form was far from perfect, but she did it.

"Wow! That was great!" I said, giving her a thumbs-up.

Toulane gave Sierra a sideways glance but said nothing. She had been acting kind of mean this week—ever since Tasha's accident. I wondered if she was stressed out about her sister. Or was she just being her usual competitive self?

We rotated to the bars and gathered around the chalk pit, a big bowl of powder that helped keep our palms from sticking on the bar.

"McKenna," Toulane said loudly, catching me off guard, "where exactly are you going when you leave class early?" She glanced around at the rest of our group as we rubbed our hands in the white powder.

Everyone stared at me, waiting for my answer.

"I bet you're getting special coaching for your routines, aren't you?" Toulane pressed on.

I didn't know what to say. I wasn't going to tell everyone about being tutored.

But Toulane wouldn't let up. "That's it, isn't it?" she said. "You're working at getting ahead of everyone else." I knew "everyone else" meant *her*.

"No, that's not it," I said firmly.

"Toulane, I don't think she wants to talk about it," Sierra piped up.

"But we shouldn't have secrets, Sierra," Toulane snapped. "We're a team. So, c'mon, McKenna, tell us." She stared at me expectantly. The other girls waited. Sierra looked a little curious, too.

I wasn't about to tell them I was struggling with schoolwork. Besides, it wasn't anyone else's business. And yet the girls kept staring, waiting for an answer. The silence was so painful that finally, the words flew out of my mouth. "Okay. Okay, yes. You're right," I fibbed. "I can't keep it a secret any longer."

"Okay, girls, let's line up," Isabelle called, urging us to gather near the bar.

Toulane stuck close to me all the way there. "So, who's coaching you?" she demanded to know.

Why couldn't she just leave it alone? I felt

myself flushing as I conjured up a lie. "She's from out east," I whispered back. First I had cheated, and now I was lying. What was happening to me?

"Huh," Toulane almost snorted. "Must be *nice.*"

"Toulane!" Isabelle called. "You're up."

Sierra shot me a sympathetic glance as Toulane pushed past me and walked to the bar. With Isabelle spotting, Toulane flew through her routine, her eyes fierce and flashing. Now that she thought I might be getting ahead, she would be even more competitive.

*If she only knew.*

As Toulane finished her routine, her mom stood up in the stands, cheering loudly. I guess Toulane had her mom's full attention now that Tasha wasn't at the gym anymore.

And then it was my turn. After what had happened between me and Toulane, I could barely remember my routine. I had to start over—twice!

"McKenna," Isabelle finally said, "what's up today? Let's concentrate this time."

Later, while we waited our turn on beam, Toulane tried to sound all friendly. "Hey, I was wondering," she asked sweetly, "what sorts of things are you working on with your private coach?"

"Nothing much," I replied. I didn't want to

make up any more information than I already had.

"Right," Toulane shot back.

After that, she refused to speak to me—not one word through the rest of practice.

<hr>

I wished on Monday that Mr. Wu would consider changing the class seating chart, but fat chance of that. It was only the first month of school. The tension between my desk and Toulane's was as thick as a brick wall.

The clock ticked slowly toward the end of the school day. When it reached 2:30, I couldn't budge. I didn't want to feel Toulane's eyes drill through me as I walked out the door.

Finally, at 2:38, Mr. Wu glanced at the clock and then at me, tapping the face of his watch.

I gathered my things. I had no choice.

When I shuffled into the library, Josie was wheeling toward me. She looked relieved to see me, but uncertain, too.

"You're leaving?" I asked.

"I didn't think you were coming," she explained. "And it didn't feel that great just waiting here alone . . . and wondering."

"Sorry," I said. "I forgot about tutoring. My teacher had to remind me." It was sort of true.

We settled at a library table to go over my homework, but as we began, all I could think about was my growing problem at gymnastics. To take my mind off Toulane and Sierra, I imagined myself on beam—visualizing each element, performing slowly with precision, toes pointed, hands perfectly poised. I had to concentrate . . . to focus . . .

"McKenna?" Josie asked, a little too loudly.

Mr. Hornbauer glanced our way from the main desk, cleared his throat, and then returned to his computer screen.

Josie closed my social studies textbook, leaned closer, and whispered, "I don't get it, McKenna."

She caught me off guard. "What?" I asked innocently.

"You were doing so well in the last session," she said, "and I thought we were making progress, but now you seem—I don't know—almost *against* being tutored."

I stared at the table. "No, I'm not—" I protested.

"Are you sure?" she asked. "I mean, you're leaving early, showing up late, daydreaming when you need to be focusing . . ." She paused. "Do you even want to do this?"

I didn't know what to say. I didn't want to be tutored, but I really had no other choice. "Yes, I do," I said weakly.

Josie was usually so bright and determined, but now she leaned back in her chair, discouraged. "We don't have to, you know. You could work with someone else, McKenna," she said quietly. Then she added, "People sometimes think if someone can't get around physically, they're not very smart mentally, either. Is that what you think of me?"

I realized suddenly that I *had* been guilty of thinking that when I'd first seen Josie in her wheel-chair, but I sure didn't think that now. "No, Josie," I said sincerely. "It's not *you*. Honest, you're great."

"Really?" Josie asked.

I nodded. "The best tutor I've ever had," I said, only half-joking. I'd never been tutored before, but I was pretty sure that even if I had, Josie would be the best of the bunch—hands down.

Josie cracked a smile. "Uh-huh," she said, shaking her head at me.

"No, I . . . ," I started again, more seriously this time. I wanted Josie to understand what I meant, but it was hard to explain. "It's just that gymnastics comes so easily for me compared to schoolwork. I'd rather dream about gymnastics. In my head, I visualize every step of my routines, and then when I do them, everything works. I know I can do *that*—master the moves. But I don't know if I can do *this*." I stared at the homework in front of me, and my shoulders slumped. "Maybe I'm not smart enough."

Josie softened. "*I* believe you can do this," she said. "As long as you're willing to try."

I looked up at Josie. A disability sure hadn't held *her* back. She seemed so strong and confident. Honestly, I believed she could do anything she put her mind to.

I nodded. "I'll try harder," I said. "I promise." And I meant it.

"Good," Josie said. "Then let's do this—together."

Thursday afternoon, before heading to practice, I stopped at the coffee shop. As I stepped through the door, Mom glanced up, lifted her forefinger, and mouthed, "One minute." She pushed a small metal pitcher of milk under the steamer and then poured the frothy milk into a cup.

"Latte with vanilla," she said, sliding the cup in front of a woman seated at the counter. The woman smiled broadly at me as she adjusted the paisley shawl around her shoulders. "So, this is McKenna?" she asked.

Mom motioned me closer. "McKenna, honey," she said, "this is Mrs. Myers, your tutor's mother."

I crossed my arms, bewildered. "Josie?" I asked. "I mean, you're Josie's mom?" I couldn't figure out why my tutor's mother was right here, in my mom's coffee shop.

"Claire and I have met before at our Women in Business meetings," Mom explained, "so it was fun to realize that our daughters are working together."

"And moms love to talk about their kids, don't they?" Mrs. Myers said, winking at me.

I nodded. "Yup." But for some reason, the idea of Mom talking with other people about my tutoring made me feel uncomfortable.

"Of course, we talk about a few other things, too," said Mom matter-of-factly.

I nodded and forced a smile. Then I found my own place to sit toward the back of the shop.

After Mrs. Myers left, Mom came from behind the counter and sat down beside me.

"I didn't mean to embarrass you, honey," she began. "You know, Josie's mom tells me Josie *loves* working with you."

"Not always," I said doubtfully, remembering how frustrated Josie had been with me at the start of our last tutoring session.

Mom scrunched her eyebrows together, waiting for me to say more.

"Josie's great," I said. "I just never thought I'd have to get help. It makes me feel so . . ."

"What?" Mom asked, her eyes softening.

"Oh, I don't know," I said with a shrug.

Mom lightly kissed my forehead. "Honey," she said, "only *smart* people ask for help."

I wasn't so sure about that, but I felt a little better. I gathered my things and stepped into the break room—and the Maisey-Mara tornado.

★

When I met Josie on Monday, her eyes danced with energy. "Hey, McKenna," she said. "You know how you visualize your moves for gymnastics?"

"Yeah?" I answered, wondering where she was going with this.

"We're going to try something like *that* with reading," Josie announced. She held up a book titled *James and the Giant Peach*. "You've heard of this one?"

I nodded. "But I've never read it," I said.

"Even better," said Josie. "I picked this one out because I thought it would be a good one to practice visualization with. I've heard that if you make pictures in your head of what you're reading, that can really help with comprehension."

"Okay . . ." I said hesitantly. I was willing to try, because I'd promised Josie last week that I would.

Josie opened the book to the first page, and we took turns reading out loud. After reading for a while, Josie placed a tree-shaped bookmark in the book and closed it. "Let's stop for a second and think about what we've read so far. In your mind, what does James look like?"

I closed my eyes, trying to picture him. "I think he's kind of small," I said. Then I shook my head and opened my eyes. "I don't know."

"Well, let's see," Josie said, crossing her arms. "What color hair does he have? What color eyes?"

"I'm not sure," I said. I really didn't know.

"That's where this can be fun," Josie continued. "Just make it up—think about someone you already know maybe, or pick any color for his hair and eyes. We can build a picture of him together."

"Mmm. Okay," I said, squeezing my eyes shut. "How about blond hair? And brown eyes?"

"Okay. Good start—" Josie began.

"Wait!" I interrupted her. "No, now I see him as having brown hair. Yeah, brown, with brown eyes— and he's skinny."

"Okay," said Josie. I could hear the smile in her voice. "Anything else?"

"Freckles," I added. "Lots of freckles."

"Now," Josie said, "what's he wearing when he meets the insects in the Peach?"

"Oh, something dark," I said, this time with more certainty.

"Kind of like where he lives?" Josie asked.

"Yeah, just like the house—black pants and a gray shirt," I described.

"So what does the house look like?" Josie asked.

"Umm . . . maybe gray outside," I said. "With pointy windows, like triangles. There's a house on my street that has those, and when I was little, I always thought it was kind of scary-looking."

"Excellent!" said Josie.

I laughed. "Yeah, this is cool," I agreed. "I have this whole picture of what the house looks like!" Visualizing with Josie was like going to a movie. I could actually see the story in my head.

After that, we worked together to describe the insects and the inside of the Peach. We read a few more pages and then tried to picture in our minds more characters and places in the story. When we were done, Josie said, "Hey, great job today! Do you think you can try this at home and visualize as you read another chapter?"

"Yeah. I think so," I said. I was actually kind of looking forward to it. "I feel as if I know James better. He's more real to me. Now I want to read what happens next."

"Good!" said Josie. "Maybe this is something that will really help you. I hope so."

*Me, too,* I thought as I packed up to go. I was worried that visualizing wouldn't be as easy without Josie by my side, but I would try, just as I'd promised.

After Tuesday's practice, I sat down for dinner—butternut squash soup and grilled cheese and tomato sandwiches—and complained about the pile of homework I had *again.*

"Mr. Wu pushes really hard," I told my parents. "And he's strict about everything."

"He sounds like Coach Francesco," Mom said with a laugh. "He'll be your coach if you move up to the competitive team. Then what will you say?"

"That's different," I said, stirring my soup. "I mean, I *want* to be pushed at gymnastics—but not at school!"

After helping with dishes, I made myself a cup of hot cocoa. Then I settled at my desk, with Cooper at my feet and Polka Dot napping—for once—in the little round den beside her wheel. But I still couldn't concentrate.

Finally, I moved to the floor and worked on my splits stretch, thinking of how Sierra could do the splits so easily. Sierra was flexible, but she'd had to work hard to catch up on technique. Since she'd joined the gym, however, she'd already come a long way.

Maybe I could work on my homework in

the same way—one step at a time—and hope for progress. I took my homework to the floor and stretched while I read.

The next day after school, I biked through a misty drizzle to the Queen Anne Public Library.

Josie and I had arranged to meet at the public library instead of in the school library. Josie had a surprise up her sleeve, as usual.

I locked my bike under a giant cedar, and then I scaled the stone steps. I wondered for a moment how Josie had gotten into the library. This main entrance, with all its steps, sure wouldn't work for her. Then I remembered there was a basement entrance on the other side that led to an elevator.

I was relieved to find Josie waiting for me in the lobby. She was all smiles. "McKenna," she said brightly, "let's have some fun!"

I wasn't sure that being at the library was my idea of *fun*, but I was willing to go along.

I followed Josie in her wheelchair—she could get around pretty fast!—to the children's reading room. She wheeled up to the picture-book area. I stood there, hoping no other kids my age were nearby.

How embarrassing to be in the baby section—with a tutor!

"Let's pull out picture books," she said, "and then chapter books. Show me your favorites, and I'll show you mine. We'll sit and read a few."

I groaned. "But they're too easy," I complained.

"Sometimes it's good to go back to easy," said Josie. "When I get frustrated, I remind myself there was a time when I couldn't tie my own shoes or make my own bed."

I nodded—that made sense. I turned to the low rack of picture books. I recognized several of them, and then I came across an old favorite.

"Oh, I loved *Harry, the Dirty Dog*!" I whispered loudly, nudging Josie. I flipped the book open and read it cover to cover, standing right there in the library aisle. "That *was* easy," I said as I slid the book back onto the shelf.

"Good! That's the point," said Josie. "Let's read a bunch of them."

Soon I'd gathered an armful of books, plopped into a green beanbag chair, and started turning pages. "You're right," I admitted after reading another book. "This is fun."

Then we turned to the chapter books on nearby

shelves. Josie showed me one of her favorite series, the *Little House* books. I showed her the *Judy Moody* series that I'd read last year. It was a big boost to see how easy that series looked to me now. Josie was right—I *had* come a long way.

Though I blinked away fat raindrops as I biked home, I rode up and down the hilly streets with a new sort of confidence. Like a hot-air balloon, I would soar high above my schoolwork problems. I visualized a brightly striped balloon floating above the mountain peaks as I hummed the music from my gymnastics routine.

But when I returned home, my balloon started to deflate. I had lots of homework to do, and none of it was as easy or as fun as the picture books I'd just been reading. By the time I got settled at my desk after dinner, I was tired. I wanted to do anything *but* homework. Down, down, down I sank.

I did math problems and then turned to my science textbook. My eyes glazed over.

What if my grades *didn't* improve? What if I had to pull back on gymnastics?

"Mom . . ." I moaned, as if I'd just crashed into the mountain.

She poked her head through my doorway, a novel in her hand. "What is it, honey?" she asked.

"Can you keep me company?" I pleaded.

Mom nodded. "Dad's reading to the twins," she said. "Think you'd like to work with a little music?"

"Maybe," I said.

Mom returned with a Mozart CD and popped it into my CD player. "I don't know if it'll help you or make things harder," she said, "but I find I read better with background music. Let's see if you do, too."

"Mozart?" I asked. "That might put me to sleep."

"It also might help you concentrate better," Mom countered. She pushed Play. Then she climbed the ladder up to my bed with her book and flipped on the reading light.

Mozart's music seemed to fill my bedroom with warm sunshine and energy. I could visualize it: bright blue sky *in* . . . soggy gray sky *out*.

To my surprise, the music helped me focus, though it seemed to put Cooper to sleep beside me.

Finally, though it was hard, I finished the last of my homework—on my own. I wasn't sure I had gotten everything right, but I'd done my best.

I stood up, stretched, and stood on my tiptoes to peek at Mom. She was sleeping, her book lying open on her chest. I gently nudged her.

"Oh dear!" said Mom, sitting up quickly. "Did I oversleep?"

I shook my head. "No, Mom," I giggled. "It's time for bed."

Mid-bite through my buttermilk pancakes the next morning, Dad announced, "Girls, we're taking the weekend off—from everything."

I set down my fork. "But I have practice on Saturday," I reminded him.

"Your mom is getting extra help at the coffee shop, and we're all heading to the Olympic Peninsula for a little hiking, biking, and hanging out together," Dad continued, as if he hadn't even heard me.

"Yippee!" Maisey said.

Mara joined in, her mouth full. "O-wimpic Powin-sow-uh?" she mumbled.

But what about gymnastics? Didn't anyone care about that?

I glared at the twins. A drop of syrup dotted Maisey's chin. "It's Olympic Peninsula, Mara," I corrected her. "And don't eat with your mouth full."

Dad laughed. "Now look who's talking, McKenna," he teased. "I believe it's 'don't *talk* with your mouth full.'"

I refused to meet Dad's eyes as I finished my pancakes and sausage links. If Mom were home, she'd stand up for me. But after breakfast, I tried again.

"Dad, I really need to practice," I insisted. "The demonstration isn't far off now."

"I realize that," he said as he poured himself more coffee. "But you know, honey, it's *actually* 'Family first, school second, and gymnastics third.'"

I couldn't win—not if what was important to me kept getting pushed to the bottom of the list. And though I wanted to argue, I could tell this was something that was already decided.

As I packed up my backpack, I sighed, thinking about a weekend away. I wouldn't admit it out loud, but I *had* been pushing myself pretty hard lately between gymnastics and school. Maybe a break wasn't such a bad idea.

"Dad, if I have to go, can I invite a friend along?" I asked. I thought about inviting Sierra, until I remembered she'd be at practice on Saturday. Maybe I could ask Elizabeth.

"Actually," said Dad, clearing the plates from the table, "your mom said the Myers family might join us. They'll rent their own cabin. It'll be fun."

"Josie Myers? Dad, she's in a wheelchair. How's *that* going to work?" I asked. The words came out sharper than I'd intended.

Dad set a plate in the sink and then walked

back to me. He rested his hands on my shoulders and pecked the top of my head. "I'm not sure how it will work," he said, "but I'm confident that Josie's family will figure things out. Now, you'd better hustle and catch that bus."

———————★

That night at gymnastics, I worked hard on my floor routine. I waited until the music started up and then propelled myself forward, letting the music fill me and flow through my body. I did a split jump and then, without hesitation, flowed into my handstand forward roll.

I launched into a leap, hop, and split—trying to stay focused on the moves and the music—but I couldn't stop thinking about the weekend ahead. I couldn't believe my parents had made all those plans without checking with me.

As I executed a perfect back roll to push-up position, I thought about Josie. She was great, but the tutoring sessions were hard work—and I had never thought of Josie as someone I could just hang out and have fun with away from school. Plus, she was older than I was. Would she even want to hang out with someone my age? To top it all off, I'd been looking forward to Saturday's practice so that I could sharpen my routine alongside Sierra, who had really been improving lately. Now I'd be falling behind.

Behind at school. Behind at the gym. Yippee.

I neared the end of my routine and threw myself into the last element, the round-off back handspring rebound.

"McKenna!" I suddenly heard my little sisters call to me from a nearby mat, where their group was working.

I lost my focus and faltered, sprawling shoulder-first into the mat instead of "sticking" my landing.

I glared at the twins and smacked the mat with my hand. "Hey!" I scolded. "You two made me fall!"

Isabelle was at my side instantly. "Are you okay?" she asked, extending her hand toward me.

"Yeah," I muttered. I stood up and shook out my arms.

"Girls," Isabelle said to Maisey and Mara, "focus on what your own group is doing. You can visit with your sister later."

Then she turned to me. "McKenna, you've heard 'There is no *I* in *team*'?" she asked.

I nodded. I wanted to say, *a thousand times.*

"Well," Isabelle continued, "there is no *mean* in

*team* here, either. Your sisters shouldn't have distracted you, it's true. But *you* need to work on sportsmanship, and that means never blaming some-one else, even when you're sure it's not your fault. Understand?"

I nodded again. For a second I remembered Josie's words, too, about not blaming other people for our own problems and mistakes. Funny how often her words came to mind at the gym. "I'm sorry," I said to Isabelle.

And that was when I made a decision. It was time to push back my shoulders, quit taking out my frustration on others, and make the best of the week-end ahead.

———————★

Josie had suggested once that a good way to practice my reading skills was to read aloud to someone else, so I decided that night to read to my little sisters. Plus, I felt bad that I'd snapped at them at the gym. I mean, sometimes I forget that they're only five.

"Careful," I said as they climbed up the ladder to my bed. I leaned against the wall and patted either side of me. "One here, and one here."

As my sisters snuggled in beside me, they were quiet, I think, for the first time in their whole entire lives.

With the comforter tucked in around us, I read to them from *Charlotte's Web*. The opening alone—"Where's Papa going with that ax?"—would be enough for any reader to predict that something terrible was about to happen. As I read, I found that the more drama I used in my voice—high and low, loud and soft, and different voices for Fern, Wilbur, and the other barnyard creatures—the more Maisey and Mara pressed up next to me.

At times I paused to ask my sisters, "Can you see Wilbur?" or "Can you imagine what this scene looks like here?" I felt as if I was playing "tutor" with them. But it helped me, too, to visualize as we were reading together.

Before I knew it, we'd finished two chapters. Finally I said, "Okay, it's bedtime."

"Noooo!" my sisters both whined, which I took as a compliment.

"Read some more!" said Maisey.

"Will you read to us tomorrow? Please?" begged Mara.

"Only if you add sugar on top," I teased.

Together the twins shouted, "Please with sugar on top!"

"How much sugar?" I asked.

My sisters knew our family drill. "Heaps and heaps and heaps of sugar!" they answered happily as they piled on top of me.

# Chapter 9

# The Waterfall

Not everyone rides ferries to get from place to place, but we do. Because Seattle is surrounded by water, peninsulas, mountains, and islands, ferries take us where bridges and roads can't.

On Friday afternoon, the line of traffic waiting for the ferry was long. But finally Mom drove our black Subaru onto the boxy boat of steel. The orange-vested attendant motioned us forward between white lines, right behind Josie's family's van. Though it's only a thirty-five-minute crossing to the Olympic Peninsula, we jumped out of our parked car and headed up the stairs to the deck.

I glanced back at the van. "Mom, aren't Josie and her parents coming up?" I asked.

"I'm not sure, honey," Mom said as she reached for my sisters' hands.

Above deck, I led the twins over freshly buffed floors, past the cafeteria and rows of cushioned benches. We wound by tourists speaking foreign languages and finally headed out the swinging doors to the open deck.

A haze hung above the horizon, blocking views of Mount Olympia and Mount Rainier. A chill, damp wind whipped my hair, but I didn't mind.

"Picture time," Dad said, camera ready.

The twins and I clustered against the railing with Mom. *Click.*

As I stepped away from the railing, I noticed an elevator near the top of the stairs. "Mom," I blurted, "Josie could take that to get up here!"

Mom seemed uncertain. "Maybe it's too much work for a short ferry ride," she said.

That was probably true. I felt bad for thinking it, but I suddenly wished that Sierra, instead of Josie, had been able to join me for this trip—someone who could be on deck with me instead of down below.

The railing was cold, but I rested my chin on my arms and gazed out. The ferry sounded its horn. Across the bay, Bainbridge Island was a cluster of bug-sized boats and houses, growing larger as the ferry chugged through swells.

Water sprayed white against the hull below. My thoughts drifted as I scanned the bay, looking for whales. I'd seen them once before, when I was seven. I probably wouldn't see any today, though, because they migrate north in the spring, not in the fall.

*Spring*—the season when I hoped to join the competitive team at Shooting Star. I thought of Sierra and Toulane, who would be practicing tomorrow— without me. My mood plummeted like the seagulls and cormorants swooping low over the water.

When I'd told Isabelle I'd be gone for the weekend, she had just smiled and said, "That's fine, McKenna. You have a great time with your family." I doubted Chip Francesco would be as easygoing with his competitive team.

I brooded as the ferry hummed along.

Speakers blared: "Passengers with cars, return to your vehicles and prepare to unload." I pushed away from the railing and followed my family back down the stairs.

Before hopping into our car, I knocked on the window of the Myerses' van. Mrs. Myers unrolled the window so that I could talk to Josie.

"How was it up top?" Josie asked.

"Great!" I said. "On the way back, you should take the elevator up. It's worth it."

"Okay," said Josie with a grin. "I'll check it out."

I hurried back to our car, and soon we were on the road, driving to Port Angeles. Ancient trees, thick with moss and ivy, surrounded us. Dabs of red and gold leaves clung to branches. With each turn, the road grew narrower.

At last, we turned in at a wooden sign that read *Whispering Pines Lodge*. A winding gravel road led us alongside a mountain stream and past little cabins tucked among giant pines, thick undergrowth, and moss-covered boulders. I almost expected to be greeted by Snow White's seven dwarfs.

In this magical place, it was hard to think about schoolwork and the gymnastics practice that I was missing. I felt a rush of excitement and decided once again to make the best of the weekend. As soon as we settled into our cabin, I marched right off to Josie's, which had handicap access—a long ramp leading to the front door.

Josie answered the door wearing a fleece jacket. She looked as ready for adventure as I felt.

"Josie, do you want to explore?" I asked her. What I really wanted to ask was, "*Can* you?" I wasn't sure if her wheelchair could handle the trails around the lodge.

"Have wheels, will travel," Josie said confidently as she wheeled down the ramp.

I followed behind her and took a long, deep breath. The air smelled as spicy and sweet as ginger-snap cookies.

Without talking about where we were going, Josie and I headed for the stream. We crossed the bridge, which was wide enough for Josie's chair and had railings along the sides. Then we found a place to sit, Josie in her wheelchair and me on a moss-covered rock. I closed my eyes and soaked up the sounds. Mountain waters gurgled nearby, and a wind chime sang from somewhere near the lodge.

"I didn't expect *this*," Josie said. "I feel like we just crossed into another world."

It *was* like another world. "It's like Narnia," I said, smiling.

"Or the land of hobbits," added Josie.

"Or the bridge to Terabithia," I said with a giggle. Josie and I had visited lots of other worlds through the books we'd read together. It felt nice to sit here with her now, as if we were creating a new world all our own.

———★

That first night, our families played board games by a crackling fire. I didn't want to admit it, but I was enjoying a weekend away, even if it *did* mean missing gymnastics.

The next morning, my family and I hiked down a two-mile path marked "Nature Trail." By the time we returned to our cabin, Mara and Maisey were so tired that they fell asleep on the living-room rug.

"Mom," I whispered. "Dad's reading. Want to go for a hike, just you and me?"

"I'd be honored," she said, reaching for her jacket.

Together we followed a different trail behind our cabin. It led us around fallen trees and small switchbacks up a steep slope. When we stopped at a bluff overlooking a rippling river, I enjoyed the view, but something was bothering me. I wished Josie could be there beside me.

"Mom," I said, "I wish Josie weren't stuck in a wheelchair."

"Mm-hmm," Mom answered. Her eyes were closed, her face lifted upward.

"I wish she could see beautiful places like this, but the trail's too rough," I thought out loud. "There has to be a trail nearby that's wheelchair-friendly."

"You mean *accessible*?" Mom asked.

I nodded.

"I like the way you think, McKenna," said Mom, squeezing my shoulders. "Maybe we could go back and check some of the trail maps. There might be something nearby on the peninsula for Josie."

Shortly afterward, I trekked excitedly toward Josie's cabin. Before I even reached the door, I could hear sweet, beautiful music floating out from the cabin. I paused at the base of an orange-lichen-covered tree, listening. The music was as high and clear as a mountain stream.

When the music stopped, I stepped up to the cabin door and knocked.

Mrs. Myers met me there. "Hey, McKenna!" she said, inviting me in.

Behind her, Josie set down a silver flute. Sheet music rested on a music stand near her chair, and nearby, bright flames licked at the woodstove's glass doors.

"I didn't know you played the flute!" I said, stepping toward Josie. "That was beautiful." For all the things Josie couldn't do because of her disability, there were so many things she *could* do—and do well.

"Thanks," said Josie. As she began putting away her flute, a flush of pink color rose in her cheeks. I could tell she was proud.

"Okay, Josie," I said. "I have a surprise."

"What?" she asked immediately.

"I can't tell you. It's a *surprise*," I repeated. "But I'll need some help getting you there."

"Where?" Josie asked.

"If I told you, it wouldn't be a surprise, would it?" I said, raising my hands in mock exasperation.

My mom showed up then with a map and directions for Josie's parents. Mom spoke with them quietly in the kitchen so that Josie wouldn't overhear. I could tell by her parents' expressions that they were as excited about my plan as I was.

Josie's parents operated the lift to get Josie and her wheelchair into their van. I sat in the back beside Josie and waved good-bye to my mom through the window.

A few miles farther, we passed through the ranger's station at Olympic National Park. A ranger waved us on, and the van eased into a parking spot marked with a blue wheelchair symbol.

After we got out of the van, Mrs. Myers pulled out her binoculars and aimed them toward the branches of a nearby tree. "Go ahead," she said, nodding toward the trail. "We'll catch up."

Too excited to wait, Josie wheeled in her chair ahead of me down the paved trail. I was happy to follow. Josie stopped here and there to touch ferns and moss. "Wow, look at that leaf," she said, pointing toward a large wet leaf on the ground.

I picked it up and handed it to her. It was gigantic—three or four times the size of our hands.

"And there!" Josie exclaimed, pointing to a tree beside the trail.

I walked over to the cedar, its trunk *enormously* enormous. I stretched my arms out, just to see how far I could reach around the trunk. Not very far!

Somewhere beyond us, water gurgled and rushed. After a gentle climbing slope, we rounded a curve, and there in front of us was Madison Falls, silver droplets cascading over a carpet of vibrant moss. Mist floated up from the creek below, where water danced at the base of the falls.

"Ohhh," Josie said. "I've seen pictures, but I've never seen a waterfall up close like this. McKenna, this is the best surprise. Thank you!"

We lingered there for a while. I sat on a bench with Josie in her wheelchair beside me. I tried to watch droplets of water as they came over the crest of the ridge and follow them, down, down, down . . . But soon I couldn't help myself from eyeing the low wooden railing at the overlook, imagining what it would feel like to jump up and do my beam routine next to the waterfall. The camera would zoom in, and a commentator would say, "Here's where the national

champion practiced, right on this railing, not knowing that she would someday be a celebrated gymnast—"

"Don't even think about it," Josie said.

I turned to face her. "What?" I asked innocently.

"Using that railing as a balance beam, that's what," said Josie, giggling.

My jaw dropped. "Are you a mind reader?" I asked her. Just when I thought Josie couldn't possibly get any smarter, she surprised me again.

Josie's dimples deepened. "If *I* were you, I'd want to do it," she explained. "But *don't*, because if you fall in, I won't be much help."

I laughed and set my sights a little lower—on the ground. With the waterfall as my background music, I attempted a back walkover, but the trail was damp. My hand slipped and I fell, just as Josie's parents came around the corner. I landed in a heap, scraping my leg against the nearby railing. *Ouch.*

"Oh dear," Mrs. Myers said. "Are you okay?"

"I'm fine," I said. I jumped up and stole a glance over the railing to the six-foot drop and the rocky riverbed below. "Good thing I didn't try that on the railing," I said, my heart pounding a little.

Josie held a straight face. "Told you so," she said.

# The Waterfall

Then our eyes met and she started to laugh—and I did, too, until my sides hurt.

That night at the lodge, Josie and I read side by side on the leather couch for over an hour. I suddenly looked up from my library book, *Island of the Blue Dolphins.* "Josie, it's happening!" I said, nudging her elbow.

"What are you talking about?" she asked.

"I'm reading faster—and seeing it all in my head as I go," I explained. "I just read ten pages and I pictured everything I was reading about!"

I felt a glow as warm as the fire, as bright as the light pouring through the stained-glass lampshade.

"I knew you could do it, McKenna," said Josie sweetly.

That night at the cabin, I dreamed I was on a remote island, flying through my gymnastics routines, surrounded by soft moss, waterfalls, and lapping water.

Sunday came way too soon. Before driving to the ferry, we stopped in Port Angeles for lunch. Josie and I sat at the far end of the table—away from my little sisters, who were stuck on ordering pancakes even though breakfast was no longer being served.

"Maisey whines," I whispered, "but Mara cries. I'm not sure which is worse."

"I think you're lucky," Josie said.

"Lucky?" I asked, a little more loudly. "You're kidding, right?"

Josie shook her head. "To have siblings, I mean," she said.

"Sometimes yes," I admitted. "Sometimes no."

Then Josie surprised me. From the bag hanging from her wheelchair, she pulled out two orange journals with blue pages and set them on the table.

"What are these?" I asked her.

"My surprise for you," said Josie, beaming. "I found them at a shop in Port Angeles with my mom yesterday. They looked perfect for writing poems."

I felt a twinge in my stomach. "I'm not very good at writing poems," I confessed.

"I didn't used to think I was either," said Josie, "but now I think it's fun. Plus, my teacher says that writing can help with reading. We could try writing a few poems and reading them to each other."

I didn't know what to say. I appreciated the gift, but it made me nervous, too. My reading skills were getting stronger, but I was no poet.

"We can start with haiku, which is easier than it sounds," said Josie. "It's only three lines: five syllables, seven syllables, and five syllables."

"Five, seven, five," I repeated. At first I was stuck, but then I thumped out the syllables with my hand on the table. "And we can write anything?"

"Anything," echoed Josie.

While the twins colored and the adults chatted, I opened up the book of empty pages. I could at least give haiku a try. Josie started writing in her book as I wrote in mine. I kept tapping out the rhythm of the syllables, which made it easier—almost fun.

After a few minutes of writing, Josie and I set down our pencils. "Okay, read yours first," I urged.

Josie leaned toward me and read quietly, as if sharing a secret:

> Silver notes of flute
> float above a metal chair,
> set my feet dancing.

"I *really* like that!" I praised Josie. "You're good at this!"

"Thanks," said Josie, blushing. "Your turn."

I drew in a breath and said, "Okay, but mine isn't going to be as good."

"It's not a competition," Josie reassured me. "Go ahead."

I cleared my throat, a little nervous. It was one thing to throw myself into my gymnastics routines and hope to do well, but this was different. It was so personal, like leaving my fingerprints on the page.

"Okay, here goes," I began. And then I read:

Empty pages wait
to be filled with words by two
new friends, you and me.

"Oh," Josie said, emotion playing at the edges of her eyes. "McKenna, that's so sweet! Thank you."

I was a little startled to see that my words—simple words on paper—could mean something special to Josie. "Thank *you*," I said to her, "for the journal. I love it." As I closed the orange leather cover, I thought of the many poems I'd write to fill the pages of the journal, now that I knew I could.

———————★

Tuesday at the gym, I soared, leaped, and tumbled through my floor routine with a "top of the world" attitude. A little time away hadn't hurt me. Once again, I felt like that hot-air balloon floating high above the mountains. I'd had such a great weekend with Josie, and my reading was improving. Plus, I'd almost polished my routines for the gymnastics demonstration just two weeks away.

As I finished my routine—chin up and arms out—Grandma clapped silently for me from her seat next to Grandpa.

"Okay, girls," Isabelle said. "Let's move to beam next. Sierra, you're up first."

I loved how Sierra's confidence was blooming, too. At first she had slumped a bit at the gym, as if apologizing for her height, but now she stood tall, facing the beam. She jumped up onto it, nimble as a cat, and moved through her routine.

"Girls, notice that her head is held high, toes pointed," said Isabelle. "See her hands, like a dancer's. All elements are working smoothly together."

Sierra's routine had come a long way. She appeared so sure, so confident. As she prepared to dismount, I held my breath.

Sierra didn't quite stick her landing, but Isabelle praised her routine. "Well done!" she said. "You've really improved, Sierra. Do you have any pointers for the rest of the girls?"

Toulane shot me a glance of surprise.

"Um," Sierra said, "I just kept practicing over and over, but actually"—she glanced at me— "McKenna helped a lot."

I looked up, startled.

Isabelle asked, "And how did she help you?"

"She reminded me to take my routines slowly, one step at a time," said Sierra, smiling. "And to breathe."

I was proud—and pleased—to learn I'd helped Sierra. And now that Sierra's routine was so polished, I had work to do if I didn't want her to pass me up! I had to perform well at the demonstration, too.

I glanced at Grandma, my biggest fan. I'd have to work extra hard until each element of my routine sparkled, as polished as the star pendant Grandma had given me.

———★

The next week flew by, and by Monday of the

second week, all I could think about was Saturday's demonstration. So when Mr. Wu handed out a book to read, I started to sort of panic.

"Class, I want you to read this book and, by next Monday, turn in a one-page report telling me what you read," he instructed.

A book report due in a week? What if I couldn't even finish the book by then?

Mr. Wu walked from desk to desk, handing out copies of the book. He paused at my desk and said, "I thought you might like this one, McKenna."

I turned the book over to its cover: *No Greater Dream: A Collection of Stories About Great Athletes.*

"Hmm. Looks interesting," I said—*and long,* I thought as I thumbed through the book. A total of eighty-eight pages. In one week? There were a lot of pictures, but still—there was no way I could get ready for Saturday's demonstration, plus read the whole book and turn in a report by next Monday.

I reminded myself that I'd come a long way already this year. My reading was improving, and I'd been able to get through my homework more easily. But how much homework would Mr. Wu pile on top of the book report this week?

I chewed the inside of my lip, worried. To calm

myself, I repeated in my head: *One step at a time.*

With this assignment, the first step meant cracking open the book and reading the first page. *I can do this*, I told myself. *One page at a time.*

⸻★

Wednesday afternoon, I was looking forward to meeting with Josie. I'd written a few new haiku that I wanted to share. But first, I spread out my homework, including the *No Greater Dream* book.

"Looks like you want to get right to work. What's changed?" Josie teased.

"The demonstration is this weekend," I explained. "The more I can get done right away, the better. Can we go over this worksheet first?"

Just as we started in, a familiar voice broke the silence, setting me on edge like the sound of nails down a chalkboard.

"So this is your secret gymnastics coach, huh?" It was Toulane, with Sierra at her side and hall passes dangling around their necks.

Toulane crossed her arms and glared at me. "You're not getting help with gymnastics, McKenna, *are* you?" she said in an accusatory tone.

I didn't answer.

"I can't believe you *lied* right to our faces," Toulane continued.

I wanted to disappear—*poof!* But there I sat, feeling terrible. "I didn't lie," I began. "I mean, I did— but I never meant to. You kept guessing I was getting help with gymnastics, so I finally just agreed with you." I had to admit, though, I'd done more than just agree. I'd kept the lie going much longer than I should have.

Toulane looked at Sierra, rolled her eyes, and turned back to me.

To try to soften things, I said, "This is Josie. She's been tutoring me with schoolwork. And these are my teammates from Shooting Star—Toulane and Sierra."

Toulane acted as if she didn't even see Josie, which made me mad. Josie wasn't invisible. She was sitting right there.

"Hi," Sierra said to Josie, but I could tell her heart wasn't in it.

"You guys, please don't tell anyone about me being tutored," I pleaded. "It's personal—that's why I didn't tell you before."

That set Toulane off again. Her nostrils flared, and then she spun away and walked off.

Sierra lingered. She wound strands of red hair around her finger, looking more hurt than angry. "I don't get it," she said. "I shared some personal things with you, McKenna. You could have told *me* the truth. You didn't need to lie."

"I was too embarrassed," I said, trying to make Sierra understand. "I'm sorry. I really am." Tears burned at the edges of my eyes, but I clenched my jaw, the way I'd learned to do when I fell at the gym and had to jump up and keep performing.

Sierra shrugged, and then she left, too.

I took a few deep breaths.

"That was pretty awful," Josie said.

I nodded and put my head down on my crossed arms. "I don't know if they'll get over this," I groaned. "At least not anytime soon. And the demonstration is only a few days away. Now it's going to be *so* weird!"

Josie rested her hand on my arm and asked gently, "Do you want to keep studying?"

"Not really," I said truthfully. "But putting off my homework isn't going to make things any easier. So . . . yes." I took a deep breath and tried to smile. "Thanks, Josie."

Saturday was a rain-spitting, drizzly day.

All morning, I was a jumble of nerves. I had worked so hard to keep up at school and with practice, and suddenly this was it—demonstration day. I went over and over my Level 4 routines, visualizing every hand position and imagining myself sticking every dismount.

With each rush of butterfly wings in my stomach, I reminded myself to breathe:

*Blue sky in.*

*Gray sky out.*

I tried to *feel* a flawless routine, but all I kept feeling was the thorny discomfort between me and Toulane and Sierra. Ever since they'd found me in the library, they'd acted distant.

Under Isabelle's and Chip's direction, we all got busy setting up for the demonstration. As we hustled around the gym setting up chairs, Toulane walked ramrod straight, as if performing. Sierra was talking to herself, and I knew she was reviewing her routines. They didn't have much to say to me, and I honestly didn't know how to make things better, so I didn't say anything either.

The first spectators to take their seats were Grandma, Grandpa, Mom, Dad, and the twins. I'd invited Josie, but she had to play at a flute recital. At least I had family here. I was relieved to see them, but they made me a little nervous, too. I didn't want to mess up in front of people who cared about me.

The rest of the seats filled quickly as our team of ten girls sat cross-legged on the mat, waiting for Level 4 to be called. We would perform ahead of the competitive team.

Finally, Isabelle stood at the microphone, introducing herself and Chip Francesco. Isabelle's words flew over my head in a blur, and then she extended her arm, introducing each of us by name.

"Toulane Thomas!"

"Sierra Kuchinko!"

One by one, we stood and marched forward.

"McKenna Brooks!"

As I stood among my teammates, I tried to focus on my routines ahead, not on how anxious I was feeling. We were each going to demonstrate our best routines in one or two areas. I was doing beam and floor.

Toulane chalked up first and attacked the low bar. She flew through her routine with amazing power and speed—even more than usual. When she dismounted, her mother stood up and whistled through her fingers. Toulane bounced back to our group, her face flushed with pride.

Sierra whispered to her, "You aced that!"

"Thanks!" said Toulane.

"Nice job," I managed, wishing I felt closer to the two of them.

The other girls' routines flew by, and before I knew it, Sierra was up on floor. She stood perfectly poised in the corner of the mat, waiting to begin.

When the music started, Sierra sparkled. She jumped high, flexed perfectly for the split jump, and with a burst of energy, completed her back handspring rebound. Though she finished on one foot, tottering a little off balance, her overall routine was crisp and graceful. She hurried back to the mat, smiling broadly, and sat down beside us with a sigh of relief.

Toulane leaned in toward her and said, "Sierra, that was amazing!"

I nodded at Sierra, too, and tried to smile, but given my nerves, I couldn't muster up more of a compliment.

And then I was up next, knowing my family's eyes were all on me.

Determined to turn my "butterflies" into

wing-beating energy, I jumped up on the beam and struck my pose: Toes pointed. Hands like a ballerina's. Graceful. *Energy under control.*

And then I began. My body knew what to do. It was a paintbrush, painting what I visualized— painting what I'd practiced.

I performed a high leap, followed by a handstand. I found extra height in my straight jump and landed solidly on the beam, as if I was born for this. I breathed in deeply, preparing for the dismount, shoulders back and head high. Everything so far felt perfect!

*Perfect! Except what Toulane and Sierra now think of me.*

I tried to push the thought out of my mind and focus on my dismount. The side handstand quarter turn—*perfect . . .*

. . . until I turned in the air and came down, somehow off balance and on the edge of my left foot. Instead of tumbling to absorb the fall, I spilled sideways, twisting and falling.

*Crack!*

I heard it as a searing heat zinged through my ankle.

Everything around me blurred and then went

black, and someone was screaming. When I opened my eyes, I was hunched in a ball, my left ankle sticking out at an odd angle. And then I realized it was me—*I* was the one who was shrieking.

Isabelle was instantly at my side. "Hang in there, McKenna," she said soothingly. "Don't try to get up."

I was crying from pain, but the pain seemed like nothing compared to the disappointment. An injury meant being sidelined. I tried to get up to prove that I wasn't hurt, but I immediately buckled back down into a ball.

"You're not going anywhere, McKenna," Dad said, his face suddenly close to mine. "Now just lie still until we can get you to the hospital."

Grandma hovered overhead, too. "Oh," she said, "it's already swelling like a melon."

I moaned, "It *can't* be broken!"

Then I closed my eyes again, wishing away the pain.

———————★

When Dr. Hartley returned to the exam room, she pointed to the screen and a bluish skeletal image of my foot and ankle.

"Is it broken?" I asked, already guessing the answer.

"Indeed it is," she said. "Looks like you'll be sporting a fashionable cast for a while."

"How long will I have to wear it?" I asked immediately, my voice breaking. What did it matter now that I'd made progress at school? My dream for making the competitive gymnastics team was coming to a screeching halt.

I couldn't meet Dr. Hartley's somber eyes, so I concentrated instead on her silver earrings. "Your cast will come off just as soon as you've healed," she said matter-of-factly, "and not a day sooner. I've seen some athletes who want to get back to their sport faster than they should, putting their bodies at risk. I'm not making any promises. We'll take X-rays again in two months, and then we'll see."

"Two months?" I said. That meant mid-January. I'd be behind by two months of practice—with only two months left to catch up before the spring competition. "That can't be right," I whined. "That's too long!"

Dr. Hartley raised her brows at me as if I were a toddler.

Despite my protests, I returned home on crutches with a cast around my lower leg. I felt depressed and grouchy—positively stormy. I wanted to be angry at someone, but who? The doctor—who was only trying to help me? My parents—for bringing me to the hospital? Josie was right. It never helped to blame others. That left only me to blame. If I had concentrated on my routine and hadn't let the friction with Toulane and Sierra get to me. If, if, if . . .

When we returned home, Mom and Dad set up a cot in my room. I wanted more than anything to climb up to my loft bed and hide away from everyone and everything. But right now, the ladder to my bed looked like the highest mountain in the world. I lay down on the cot and cried.

After a few hours of being pampered, I was so crabby that the only one who wanted to stay with me was Cooper. He loved me no matter what mood I was in. And when I scratched his belly, he stretched and groaned, happy to just be.

I wasn't sure when I'd ever be happy again.

I hobbled toward the bulletin board above my desk and reached for the letter that had arrived from Shooting Star Gymnastics before the start of school. I read it aloud to Cooper.

*Congratulations, McKenna! We're pleased to let you*

*know that you have been invited to the Twisters in Level 4.*
*You are also on track for the competitive team next spring.*
*We wish you every success!*

I closed my eyes, remembering how excited I had been when the letter first arrived. Now, though, thinking about that exciting opportunity caused a lump in my throat.

I folded the letter back into thirds and tossed it onto my desk.

"Looks like I'm on the slow track now," I said sadly. Cooper looked up at me and whined.

I remembered the Mozart CD that Mom had brought into my room a couple of weeks ago. It was still in my CD player. I pushed Play, just to see if the music might help lift my foul-weather mood. In contrast, the notes were bright and nimble, lively as . . . as a gymnast.

As the music filled my room, I replayed my beam routine in my mind, remembering how everything had flowed perfectly—until I lost my concentration. Until I thought about Sierra and Toulane . . . and fumbled my dismount.

I moped, toying with the chain of my silver necklace.

## Smack, Crack


Finally, I reached for my journal with the orange cover and opened it to the first blank page. I stared at the page, twirling my pencil. It wasn't easy, but I made myself write—word by word.

As I wrote what I felt, what I had visualized, my feelings began to slowly untangle:

> Twirling, leaping high,
> muscles work to reach the sky.
> Then smack, crack—off track.

Sometime before dinner, I heard knocking on my bedroom door.

"Special delivery!" announced Grandpa.

Before I could say, "Come in," the doorknob turned and the twins bounded into my bedroom with Grandma and Grandpa close behind. I was still sitting at my desk, my foot elevated as the doctor had ordered.

Mara and Maisey both gripped a basket wrapped with iridescent pink paper.

"We took the twins shopping," Grandma said.

"It's from me," Mara said.

"And me," Maisey added.

"Open it!" they said in unison.

I peeled off the fluff of silver ribbon and unwrapped what was in the basket. It was an adorable stuffed panda with the sweetest eyes.

"Oh!" I squealed. "It's so cute!" I gave each of my little sisters a kiss on the cheek.

"He can keep you company," Maisey said.

"I have a name for her," Mara added.

"Her? It's a girl bear?" I asked.

"Uh-huh," Mara answered confidently. "And I think you should call her . . . Panda."

I couldn't help but smile. "Panda," I repeated.

"Mara, that's absolutely perfect."

———————★

That evening, Mom insisted that I join the whole family for popcorn and a movie in the living room.

"But, Mom, I just want to sit in my room," I protested.

"You've been in there all day, McKenna," said Mom. "You need to join us. C'mon, honey."

And she was right. Watching a movie helped me get my mind off my leg—and improved my mood. When the phone rang, Maisey jumped up to get it.

"McKenna! It's for you!" she declared, handing me the phone.

My family put the movie on pause, and I took the call. It was Josie. "Oh, hi!" I said.

"I'm sorry you got hurt," Josie said sweetly. "But I know you'll be back on your feet soon."

"Thanks," I said to my friend. Then it hit me that Josie could never look forward to using her legs. "I wish you could get better, too," I said softly.

There was a pause, and I hoped I hadn't said something wrong.

"I'm getting better every day," Josie finally said.

"You are?" I asked. For just a moment, I felt a flash of hope that she'd found the cure for her disability.

"Not my legs, but on the inside," she said. "I'm getting better at being happy with who I am, at just being me—Josie."

I studied my cast, which had already been signed by everyone in my family. I used to think that I was all about gymnastics, but for the next few months, I'd have to focus on other things. Like Josie, I would have to work on just being me. *McKenna.*

———————★

On Sunday afternoon, Toulane called to see how I was doing. It was kind of an awkward conversation, since we hadn't really talked since she'd found out about my tutoring. But it was nice that she reached out to say hello. And later Sierra called, too, and asked if she could come over.

Half an hour later, under a ray of sunshine, Sierra showed up on our doorstep with a gift wrapped in golds and blues.

"Open it," Sierra said a few minutes later, when we were sitting together in my bedroom. She hugged her knees to her chest as I opened the box.

Nestled in tissue wrap, I discovered a tiny hand mirror, its wooden frame brightly painted.

"It's beautiful," I said. I had never imagined I needed such a thing until I held it in my hands.

"I painted it," Sierra said. "My mom's an artist. She sells things like this at Pikes Place Market. But this one—this one I painted all on my own."

"You're good," I said, turning the mirror over and over in my hands.

"It's an encouragement mirror," explained Sierra.

"Yeah?" I said. I studied the mirror, seeing only my tawny hair and my blue eyes staring back. "How does it work?"

"Well, it's like this," said Sierra. "When you look into this mirror, you can tell yourself only *good* things, not bad. Like how amazing you did at the demonstration or how you're going to heal up fast— things that *encourage* you. You've helped me so much at the gym, McKenna. I want to help you, too."

I couldn't speak for a moment—my throat felt too tight. Finally I looked up at Sierra. "Thank you," I said sincerely. "That's really, really nice."

Then Cooper nosed my door open and made himself at home right between us.

"Watch out," I warned Sierra. "He gives kisses."

Cooper stole a lick of Sierra's chin—and mine, too—and then flopped onto his back, belly up for scratching. Sierra laughed, and I joined her. It felt so good to feel good!

"Sierra," I said before she left, "I want you to know that I'm sorry. I should have told you and Toulane that I was getting tutored."

Sierra shrugged. "At first I was hurt," she said. She looked up, as if searching for the right words on the ceiling. "I mean, I'd told you how hard it was to be the biggest girl on the team, and that my parents got divorced. So I felt bad that you didn't tell me about your tutor. Besides, there's nothing wrong with getting help, McKenna. That's a really good thing, I think."

I drew a breath, exhaled, and let my shoulders relax. "I was so embarrassed," I explained, "and then when Toulane thought I was getting help with gymnastics, it was just easier to lie. But I wish I'd been brave enough to tell the truth. I'm sorry for lying, Sierra. It won't happen again. I really want to be *friends*."

Sierra smiled. "Me too!" she said happily.

On Monday I stayed home in my pajamas, my leg propped up to keep the swelling down. The only thing I could do was read, which was good, because I hadn't finished the book that Mr. Wu had assigned last week. As I read, Cooper rested his head on my lap.

The book was pretty interesting. *Thank you, Mr. Wu!* I learned that many athletes face injuries and setbacks. I pictured the athletes as I read, and that helped me focus. The pages flew by. I finished page eighty-eight *just* before falling asleep.

———★

The next morning, Grandma drove up in her Jeep. She helped me with my backpack and crutches as I climbed into her car. She was now my official chauffeur to school, the coffee shop, and gymnastics—at least until I mended.

As soon as I got to school, I hobbled into Mr. Wu's room and right up to his desk.

He looked up, eyes wide, and said, "Well, well. I got the message that you were injured, McKenna. What happened, exactly?"

I filled him in quickly and then said, "I'm sorry, Mr. Wu. I didn't expect to get hurt this weekend. I didn't get the book report done."

"That's understandable," said Mr. Wu. "But did you get a chance to *read* the book?" he asked.

"I did. And I really liked it!" I answered.

Mr. Wu smiled and nodded toward my desk. "Well, why not just sit down and write about what you liked," he suggested. "And why. You can get started now and maybe finish up after lunch. You probably need to skip recess anyway, right?"

After lunch, while the other students were outside, I worked on my report in the quiet of my classroom. At first, I didn't know what to write, but once my pencil hit the page, the words started coming. I filled up two pages with all that I wanted to say about the book. It was messy, but I reminded myself that I'd just written a "sloppy copy," or first draft.

When I finished, I almost brought the report to my teacher, but something held me back. "Mr. Wu," I asked, "will you let me work on this some more and turn it in tomorrow? I think I can make it better."

"Excellent idea, McKenna," he said right away. "Yes, of course."

———————★

That afternoon at the coffee shop, I asked Mom if I could stay with her instead of going to gymnastics with Grandma and my sisters.

"You don't want to be at the gym?" she asked. "I'm sure you can do some stretches or something."

"It's not that," I explained. "I have a book report to revise. I'll go to practice Thursday—just not today."

"Okay then," said Mom. "You can stay here if you'd like."

Skipping practice was a hard decision, but I had to do it if I was going to do a good job with my report. I sat down in the break room with the book beside me. I thought about what I'd read, what I'd liked about it, and why. Then I took a pencil to my first draft, crossed out some sentences that weren't clear, and added my new thoughts in the margins.

Later, after dinner, I typed up my report on the computer in the living room. I made changes on-screen, then fed a fresh sheet of paper into the printer and clicked Print.

I was starting to love blank pages of paper. They were a chance to start over—to begin again.

I realized that my extra efforts at writing haiku had helped me write more easily. I'd stretched my brain—and it was becoming more flexible and stronger every day. Josie was right about that, just as she was right about so many things.

The next day, before class started, I placed my report in a special blue folder on Mr. Wu's desk. Then I took my seat, knowing I had done my best work. When Mr. Wu stepped into the classroom, I crossed my fingers, hoping he'd like the report.

———★

Thursday at the gym, my teammates crowded around to sign my cast. I stretched and did sit-ups with them, but I couldn't do much else in a cast. Before long my ankle started aching.

Isabelle must have noticed. "McKenna, why don't you just rest for a bit," she suggested. "You can observe and listen in."

"I thought I could try the bar," I said hopefully.

Isabelle laughed. "Not yet," she said, shaking her head. "You'll heal, but it takes time. Be patient."

During a break, Toulane skipped over. "I'm sorry you can't practice," she said. "Gymnastics just isn't . . . well, it's not as much *fun* without you right there beside me."

It was one of the nicest things Toulane had ever said to me. I didn't know what to say.

There was an awkward silence, and then

Isabelle called Toulane back to the bars. As Toulane turned away, I found my voice. "Toulane," I called after her, "ready to work?"

Toulane gave me a warm, genuine smile. "Ready to fly," she said. As Sierra jumped up to the bar and did a hip circle, Toulane added, "I think Sierra might be ready to fly, too. My mom was talking with Coach Isabelle, and she said that Sierra might have a shot at the competitive team sometime soon."

"Really?" I said. I looked at Sierra, who was handling her routines with more confidence every day. I was happy for her, but at the same time, I felt a twinge of jealousy, too.

"You'd better hurry up and heal, McKenna, or she's going to leave us *both* in the dust!" teased Toulane. Then she darted off again to join the others circling near the chalk pit.

*How can I compete with Toulane and Sierra if I can't even work out?* I wondered. Then I caught myself. Sierra had been working hard, and more important, she was my friend. I needed to cheer for her, not compete with her.

To take my mind off the things at practice that I *couldn't* do, I rummaged around in my backpack. I pulled out the book report Mr. Wu had handed back as I'd walked out the door at the end of the day. He'd been busy with other students and hadn't said a word, so I was afraid I'd bombed the report. I wasn't sure I could handle getting a bad grade.

Finally, with lots of worry—and a little hope—I opened the blue folder. I couldn't believe my eyes.

*A+!*

I teared up and stared at the page. Never had a good grade meant so much to me. Then I read slowly through Mr. Wu's comments in the margins:

*Great summary!*
*Strong action words.*
*You could be a sports writer!*
*Nicely done, McKenna!*

Here I was, sitting on the sidelines with a broken ankle, but I couldn't keep from smiling.

When practice ended, Mara and Maisey bounded up to me. "Let's get going," I said to them. "Grandma's waiting for us."

As Grandma drove us home, the windshield wipers flapped and the twins sang in the backseat. I flipped on my reading light and pulled out my new journal.

"Homework?" Grandma asked, eyes fixed on the road.

"No, I just feel a poem coming on," I told her. "Something to post on my bulletin board."

"Why does that not surprise me, McKenna?" Grandma said jokingly.

I stared out the window. I still aimed to be on Shooting Star's competitive team. A broken ankle wasn't going to stop me. But like heavy clouds above a harbor, Toulane's words hung over me: *Hurry up and heal.* How was I going to do that?

I tapped out a rhythm and then wrote:

One step at a time.
Blue sky, blue sky, blue sky in.
Gray sky, gray sky—out!

# Letter from American Girl

Dear Readers,

American Girl receives thousands of letters every year from girls like you. Many of those letters are from girls who are struggling in school, just as McKenna is. We published McKenna's story to show how one fictional girl learns to believe in herself and bring her grades back up—and to inspire you to find ways to handle school struggles in your own life.

Read the following real letters from real girls, and learn how *you* can overcome obstacles in the classroom, too—one step at a time.

Your friends at American Girl

## PARENTS AND GRADES

Dear American Girl,
My mom expects me to get A's and B's, but on my last report card, one of my grades went from an A+ to a B-. I told her things were just getting harder, but she won't let it go. I think she expects too much.
—Under Pressure

A B— is nothing to feel bad about as long as you gave the class your best effort, but falling grades in one subject are a slippery slope. Your mom might be worried that your grades will keep dropping lower, so she wants to help you now, before you fall too far behind.

　　If the class feels "harder," try to figure out why. Is there material you don't understand? More homework? Tougher tests? If you don't know where points were lost, talk with your teacher to find out. Then ask for tips on how to improve your scores in those areas.

　　If your mom sees you working hard and asking for help when you need it, she may not push you as much about your grades. She'll feel better about your work, and so will you.

## ASKING FOR HELP

Dear American Girl,
I'm having trouble in math. How can I ask for help without feeling stupid?
—Stumped and Scared

Asking for help isn't stupid—it's *smart*. In fact, students who ask the most questions get the best grades. Ask your teacher for help right away. Everything you learn in math builds on what you learned before, so if you don't understand what's happening in class today, you'll most likely be confused tomorrow—and the next day, too.

Raise your hand and ask questions during class, or talk to your teacher right after class. If you're still confused after talking with your teacher, don't be afraid to say so. Your teacher might be able to explain things in a different way.

Remember that your teacher wants you to do well. It's his or her job to make sure you understand what's being taught, and if you don't understand, it's *your* job to speak up.

121

## CHEATING

Dear American Girl,
I can't spell. I study hard, but if I'm having trouble on a spelling test, I end up looking at someone else's paper. I know I have to stop. But if I don't copy, I'm afraid I'll fail!
—Copycat

If you do copy, you're failing anyway, right? You're failing to learn the words, so you're falling further behind. Instead, try this tip: while you're doing homework, keep a dictionary handy at your desk or online, and *use* it. Every time you look up a word and see it spelled correctly, you're helping your brain memorize it—which means that those spelling-test scores should start going up.

If you're tempted to let your eyes wander during tests, tell yourself firmly, *No! I'm doing this on my own.* You might not get perfect scores at first, but that will bother you less than a guilty conscience. And if you don't start getting the scores you want? Ask your teacher for help figuring out study tips that will work for *you.*

# DAYDREAMING

Dear American Girl,
I have a BIG imagination. Instead of paying attention in school I wander off into my imagination. Then I get confused and can't figure out where we are in class or if my teacher called on me or not. Help!
—Daydreamer

An active imagination can be a great thing. The trick is to use it to *help* you rather than hurt you. While your teacher is talking, try *visualization*, as McKenna did. Picture in your mind what you're hearing as your teacher talks. Is the lesson about wagon trains? Make a mental movie of the covered wagons in your head, and let your teacher's voice guide what happens next.

What else can you do? Get involved! Raise your hand often during class to ask questions or to comment on what you just heard. While your teacher is talking, take notes—keep your hand and pencil moving. The more involved you are in the lesson, the more interesting it will seem to you, and the less your mind will wander.

Mary Casanova loves to read, but it wasn't always that way. Though she was good at reading aloud in class, she struggled to comprehend much of what she read. She loved to check out books at the library, but as an "active, can't-sit-still, adventure-seeking kid," she found *finishing* books difficult.

Now, as the author of over two dozen books for young readers—including *Cécile, Jess, Chrissa,* and *Chrissa Stands Strong* for American Girl—she's passionate about writing stories that kids can't put down.

When Mary isn't writing—or traveling for research or to speak at schools and conferences—she's likely reading a good book, hiking with her husband and three dogs, or horseback riding in the north woods of Minnesota.